14

2

7

SE

A fiı

DEADLY CHOICE

*Christine Green titles available from
Severn House Large Print*

Deadly Bond
Deadly Echo
Fire Angels
Vain Hope

DEADLY CHOICE

Christine Green

Severn House Large Print
London & New York

This first large print edition published in Great Britain 2006 by
SEVERN HOUSE LARGE PRINT BOOKS LTD of
9-15 High Street, Sutton, Surrey, SM1 1DF.
First world regular print edition published 2004 by
Severn House Publishers, London and New York.
This first large print edition published in the USA 2006 by
SEVERN HOUSE PUBLISHERS INC., of
595 Madison Avenue, New York, NY 10022.

British Library Cataloguing in Publication Data

Green, Christine
    Deadly choice. - Large print ed. - (A Kate Kinsella mystery)
    1. Kinsella, Kate (Fictitious character) - Fiction
    2. Women private investigators - Great Britain - Fiction
    3. Detective and mystery stories
    4. Large type books
    I. Title
    823.9'14 [F]

ISBN-10: 0-7278-7494-2

Printed and bound in Great Britain by
MPG Books Ltd, Bodmin, Cornwall.

One

At six a.m. I was staring out on to Longborough High Street watching it enveloped in a warm misty haze as if the sun were shining through a muslin curtain. Jasper, a small terrier in whom I have a half share, lay splayed out on my bed like a bit-part actor showing his all.

The late August heatwave was expected to last three days. I'd seen the sea briefly the previous year but only in poor weather and now I had the urge to make the most of the last few days of summer and be beside the seaside.

My career to date, as a private investigator, has resulted in one major success – the return of a kidnapped baby who is now toddling, throwing food and chortling at my funny faces. The baby, named Katy after me, once reunited with her mother Megan, now lives in my house in Farley Wood. Megan pays a fair rent, which means I can pick and choose my cases.

My own mother Marilyn has had a striking personality change and is also living there as

5

surrogate gran. She isn't exactly the home-baked scone type, but Megan is, and between them they seem to cope very well. So well, that when I visit I feel like the maiden aunt who is indulged but is always just outside the cosy little circle.

Hubert Humberstone, undertaker or Funeral Director as he prefers to be called is both my landlord and friend. He has no physical attractions, being glum-faced, balding and twenty or so years older than me, but to me he is metaphorically both my rock and my crampons. Mountaineering though is not a hobby of his. Hubert works hard but he manages to maintain an avid interest in footwear, the higher the arch and heel the better. He's well known in local shoe shops as the equivalent of a 'bon viveur' of stiletto and towering platform shoes. His interest is totally harmless but his prune-coloured eyes have quite a twinkle if he sees a woman totter past in a pair of magnificent height. I could feel the same way about cowboy boots and a Stetson but that's not a likely sight in Longborough.

Longborough itself is a medium-size market town, a little old-fashioned, but as house prices have risen faster than dough it's become a sought-after place to live. The new residents though have to travel long distances to their workplaces and judging by the grey faces I see in the homecoming cars some of them regret the day they moved.

Social life in Longborough is not for the faint-hearted – there's a Fuchsia Club, the Women's Institute, the Mothers' Union, the Co-op choir and one of the local schools offers courses in subjects as diverse as calligraphy and yoga. Which means for a thirty-something like me an evening in front of the TV with a glass of wine and a bowl of popcorn seems like more fun.

My love life, along with my social life, is virtually non-existent. I did go out for a meal occasionally with a police inspector called David Todman who should have husband material stamped across his forehead. He's so straight I'm convinced he thinks the missionary position's exciting. If that sounds a little like sour grapes it probably is. He's been calling in to see Megan on a fairly regular basis and Megan is so naïve she probably thinks the missionary position is kneeling in church.

I'd decided by six thirty a.m. that the weather forecast of a hot and humid day was going to be accurate. I felt I needed a holiday, even deserved one. I've just completed three 'maritals', cases where, at the end, you're never quite sure if there is a winner. The first two involved women convinced their husbands were having affairs. So I stalked and photographed and sat in my car for hours on end. And eventually I had the evidence. One man was, and one wasn't, having an affair. The first, betrayed, woman reacted as though broken-hearted and somehow I felt guilty for giving her the bad news, even though she was paying me to do just that. The second woman when told her husband wasn't having an affair replied with considerable passion – 'I knew the little shit didn't have it in him. Now I'll have to find another reason to divorce him. Bastard!'

My third 'marital' was a strange woman with luminous eyes that stared from black-framed glasses. On her first visit to me she spoke in a whisper and said she came to me because of DV. I thought she meant a divine vision but she meant domestic violence. I recommended the police and her GP but she said she was convinced her Brian was seeing another woman. If she found he was, it would give her the strength to leave him. She was fairly persuasive so I took the case on.

Armed with a photograph of Brian I'd followed him one evening to a pub on the outskirts of town. Sure enough he was meeting a woman. He stood propped at the bar for nearly three hours talking to her. I sat supposedly reading a book and drinking orange juice and lemonade for that length of time. The only problem being that he was chatting between the sparse customers to a plump, pension-aged barmaid. And when he turned round I noticed he had a black eye.

I visited the loo and when I came back he'd gone. I judged the barmaid to be a kindly, chatty soul so I came clean about my reasons for sitting in a pub for three hours reading a book. Known as Babs she was quite forthcoming. 'Poor little bugger,' she'd said. 'He comes in here once a week when his nasty bitch of a wife is out. I reckon it's the only time he gets a chat with anyone. He tells me all his problems.'

'Which are?' I'd asked.

'Well, love, you saw his black eye. He spends so much time in casualty he's on first-name terms with the staff.'

'So he's not having an affair?'

Babs had thrown back her head and laughed. 'God give me strength – is that what the bitch is saying? He's more scared of women than I am of poisonous snakes. And he's bloody terrified of her. You do him a favour love – go back to his so-called wife and tell her he *is* having an affair – perhaps then she'll divorce him.'

Later, having run through all sorts of scenarios in my mind, I came to the conclusion that the truth was always the best option, especially as I didn't want his murder on my conscience. So I told his wife the truth. She smiled smugly and handed me a generous cheque. Somehow, though, I just couldn't let it rest there and the following week I was back at the pub. I guessed Babs would have told him who I was and I appeared about half an hour before closing time. This time the pub was busier and Babs bustled between pumps and optics and hardly noticed that I had drawn Brian away to an empty table.

His black eye had reduced to a mere greenish grey now. He had receding hair that left V shapes on his head and in general he was fairly nondescript except for a rather stooped frame of well over six foot. It was only when I began talking to him that the expression 'there's nowt as queer as folk' made me realize whoever coined it was a true philosopher.

Brian began by telling me of his latest injury. 'I just don't know what to do when she starts on me – she's as good with her fists as she is with her feet.' There was a note of pride in his voice. My suggestion that he could always leave her was met at first with silence and then with a plaintive excuse – 'But I still love her.' As I let him talk more I realized that not only was he as dim as a forty-watt bulb, he had one main role in life – *victim*. He revelled in the attention of Babs, the hospital staff and his GP. A cracked rib to him was a badge of honour. 'Look at me,' he seemed to be saying. 'I don't lose my cool – I'm a man.' His wife, Corinne, was always contrite afterwards and he enjoyed the extra attention and pampering. It was a mutually

10

destructive relationship but obviously fulfilled a need in both of them. Maybe one day he would tire of his frequent injuries or Corinne would go too far but somehow I doubted it. I think she was controlled enough to manipulate his injuries. Or maybe I'm being too cynical.

Anyway, 'maritals' are off my agenda for a while and as I saw the sun break through the muslin curtain I decided to find Hubert and break the news. Jasper, sensing I was leaving the room, awoke from his torpor, jumped off the bed and was hard on my heels barking excitedly for a walk. Hubert, I decided, would have to wait. Jasper's needs came first.

Outside, the air was already warm and humid. Jasper seemed to sense today was going to be different as his tail began wagging eccentrically as if in semaphore. It was then that I realized if I was going on a short holiday he would make the ideal companion. He would sleep beside me without snoring, disturb me only in the morning by gently licking my face, provide me with motivation to walk, eat my leftovers, would never argue about where we went and would be happy as long as I was with him. All he required in return was a bowl of food and water and the odd titbit. For that I had a companion who would neither tut about my calorie consumption nor notice how much I was drinking. Having sorted all that out in my mind it was only left to explain to Hubert that it was Jasper who needed to run free on some deserted beach and I was merely being altruistic.

Later that morning when I found Hubert cooking breakfast in the kitchen I told him of the sacrifice I was prepared to make on Jasper's behalf.

'I'd come with you,' he said. 'But I'm too busy. I suppose you want breakfast before you go.' He added more bacon to the grill and began cracking eggs. Hubert doesn't follow food fashions or any other fashion really. His attitude is – if your number is called, then it's called and barring accidents you'll get as long a life as you're programmed for. Eating a few extra eggs or resisting the call to sausages won't make any difference. I'm inclined to agree but I often argue with him just for the sake of seeing him animated. As he put breakfast in front of me I tried to disregard the cholesterol level while he mused aloud on a time when peasants lived on bread, cheese and ale and no one had heard of lemon grass, curry leaves, sun-dried tomatoes or polenta and when the only chef you knew was your mother.

'You're not thinking of wearing a bikini are you?' asked Hubert, abruptly changing tack.

'Why do you ask?'

He shrugged. 'I don't want Jasper running off at the shock.' His face was perfectly straight and he knew full well that I'd rise to the bait. 'I'll have you know,' I said, 'I don't look too bad in a bikini. In fact I think I look – sonsy.'

'Don't you mean saucy?'

'I do not. Sonsy means – plump, buxom, of cheerful disposition. I found it in the dictionary – I haven't just made it up.'

'I'm glad to hear it. The plump and buxom is you but I don't know about the cheerful disposition.'

'It also means *to bring good fortune.*'

'There you are then,' he said. 'Wrong on two counts.'

I didn't pursue that line any more; the trouble with trying one-upmanship on Hubert is that his brand of reality soon has me slipping on the banana skin.

After breakfast Hubert left for the first of his day's funerals telling me I could raid the fridge if I wanted to. I peered inside. It was full to overflowing. Then I rang Megan to tell her I was going away for a few days. My mother, of course, was still in bed.

'Where are you planning to go then?' asked Megan in her slow Welsh accent.

'I thought I'd look up somewhere on the Internet – Yorkshire maybe.'

'Wales is very nice,' she said. 'There's a farm near Nefyn that has a caravan.' I mumbled something to the effect that I'd think about it. I had no plans to do any such thing.

13

A caravan in a field was not my idea of a holiday and I'd been to Wales the year before. I wanted a change. We chatted for a while about Katy but as she began yelling for attention I made an excuse and rang off.

I spent the next hour on the Internet and the telephone trying to find a hotel or a guest house that would take a small terrier. Those that did take pets had no vacancies. It was beginning to look like mission impossible and the caravan in Nefyn was becoming a strong contender, although I suspected even that must be occupied during August. I rang Megan back to find she didn't know the address or the name of the farm but as Nefyn was a very small place I shouldn't have any difficulty finding it. 'So you're telling me,' I said, 'There's nuffin' at Nefyn.'

Megan's sense of humour is purely slapstick so she answered me in her usual serious way, 'There's a lovely beach there and it's very quiet and Lloyd George's grave is not too far – that's well worth a visit. Would you bring me back some bara brith if you do go to Wales?'

I promised I would and turned to Jasper, who snuggled against me. 'Come on then Jasper – we're off to do nuffin' in Nefyn.' Jasper, intelligent enough to know by my tone of voice something to his advantage was in the offing, barked excitedly. It took me twenty minutes to pack, a minute to leave a

14

note for Hubert, and we were ready to go. I was halfway down the stairs when the phone rang. I hesitated but only for a moment. If it were that important they'd ring again on my mobile.

Jasper is a great traveller. After a few watchful excited miles he lapses into a contented coma. On the way we stopped at a pub and he roused himself and we had lunch in a pub garden. It was a full stomach and the knowledge we were halfway there that finally made me feel in holiday mood and of course the warm sunshine and clear blue skies that seemed to hold the promise of more to come.

Nefyn simmered in the sunshine and did so with quietness reminiscent of a long Spanish siesta. The sandy beach boasted three families slothful under the shade of giant umbrellas and the sea was as waveless as a glass mirror. Jasper struggled with me to be free of his lead but I led him away from the three families, who, strangely in an empty beach, stayed close to each other. Further along the beach we were quite alone and I walked Jasper to the sea's edge, took off my sandals, released Jasper from his lead and let the sea creep over our feet. The water struck cold but Jasper was in doggie heaven dashing backwards and forwards excitedly. The heat and the excitement were soon too much for both of us and I sat by a grassy bank to recover and squint at the shiny sea. After fifteen minutes or so I carried Jasper to the car so that we could find either the farm with caravan or a guest house.

If there was a shop I didn't find it and there was no one on foot to ask. There were one or two B&Bs but they had no vacancies. Eventually though I found an elderly lady wearing a man's cap sitting reading in a deckchair outside an all-white bungalow.

'You want the Davis farm,' she said squinting at me in the bright sun. 'She's got a caravan in one of the fields. It's about half a mile up the main road. Turn left up the narrow road, keep on going and you can't miss it.'

The half-mile must have been a Welsh half-mile. By my reckoning it was at least half that again and the narrow road with high bushes each side seemed never-ending but from the smell I did at least know a farm was nearby. When I finally got there the farm was a grim stone building with a collie dog lying by the doorway of the farmhouse. I parked as near to the front door as possible and the dog raised its head and then lowered it again. Jasper barked for all he was worth but the collie wasn't impressed and stayed doggo. A middle-aged woman, red-faced and scowling, appeared then in the doorway. She looked the type who in the Wild West would have had a shotgun behind her back. 'Yes?'

'I believe you have a caravan for rent.'

Her face relaxed slightly and she toed the dog from the door and he moved a yard away and collapsed again in a warm heap. 'Come on in,' she said.

The kitchen seemed dark after the bright sun but it was hot. A smell of baking came from the gas cooker and in the grate a small fire glowed. She noticed my glance towards the fire but offered no explanation. 'It's two hundred a week,' she said, 'and twenty pounds deposit for bedlinen. I'd prefer it all in cash but I'll take a cheque.'

'That's fine,' I said. 'Shall I pay now?'

'If you want sheets on your bed, unless you've brought your own.'

I handed her a twenty-pound note and wrote out a cheque for the rest. From her apron pocket she produced a scrap of paper and a scrap of a pencil and then proceeded to write me out a receipt.

I was about to comment on the glorious day when she seemed to read my thoughts. 'It won't last, this weather. Take my word – make the most of what's left of today.' From the same pocket she handed me a key. 'Don't lose it and lock up when you go out. I'll get your sheets.' She disappeared and I heard her walking heavily upstairs, each stair creaking louder than the last. After a few moments she returned to hand me two candy-striped sheets and two pillowcases. 'The caravan is in the second field. Follow the path and try not to step in the cowpats.'

I thanked her and went out to collect Jasper. I'd failed to mention his existence and she stood at the door watching me with a slightly amused expression whilst the collie dog ignored us both.

I carried Jasper under one arm and the bedlinen in the other. The first field was full of cows and the second was empty apart from a caravan that might have once been cream but age and mud had withered it. It stood like a rusty old car, forlorn and forgotten and surrounded by cowpats. I toyed with the idea of asking for my money back but I guessed she'd refuse and I was feeling the effects of the heat and the long drive. Anyway by now it was late afternoon. It would have to do.

The caravan door creaked as it opened and a wave of hot musty air hit me. It smelt like a potting shed and even Jasper recoiled. Once the curtains were pulled and the windows opened at least I could see that the interior matched the exterior. A paraffin lamp and a box of matches had been placed on the Formica top of the drop-leaf table that I guessed hid the bed. There was no TV but there was a two-ring gas burner and a small oven. It was clean but very old and shabby. There were three cupboards – one contained a shower, which was so narrow I had to enter sideways; another was a clothes cupboard and the third contained an Elsan loo. A further 'room' contained a bunk bed.

'Well, Jasper,' I said, 'let's find civilization and go shopping.' He didn't argue. On the way I stopped off to see Mrs Davis. She must have seen me coming because as I approached she came out holding a basket. 'Everything all right?' she asked slyly.

'Fine, Mrs Davis,' I said, unwilling to give away the idea that a week in that caravan might just cause me to lose the will to live. 'I'm going for a drive around – where is the nearest town?'

'Pwllheli,' she said, 'and I'm not Mrs Davis. This is the Euan Evans farm.'

As I drove away the thought occurred to me that this could be the wrong farm and the wrong caravan but it was too late now – Pwllheli was calling me. It took half an hour or so of driving through twisty country roads and on arrival I soon realized that I should not have listened to Pwllheli calling. Sullen, bored teenagers hung around the bus bay. Many of the shops were boarded up. It had the look of a town that had somehow accepted that once having a holiday camp on its doorstep meant not only that it couldn't compete, but also that it should give up trying.

I found a small electrical shop and bought

a battery operated radio and from a gift shop a pack of cards, three paperback novels and a painting-by-numbers set. Then at the nearest off-licence I bought a box of red wine because there was no fridge to cool white wine. From a baker's that was about to close I purchased the last cream doughnut and then managed to find a small supermarket and bought dog food, a small cooked chicken, potatoes and runner beans, ready-prepared salad, long-life milk and assorted chocolate bars. I wasn't going to starve. For good measure I bought a selection of fruit and a packet of biscuits – Jasper loves biscuits. With these supplies the week at the caravan from hell wouldn't seem so bad.

Having wandered round Pwllheli and sat outside a pub having an orange juice I decided to drive back. Already I felt quite lonely; there were elderly couples and families but few people of my age. I supposed that if you had any ambition, a sleepy, half-forgotten seaside town was the last place anyone youngish and single would want to be.

By the time I found Nefyn and the farm dusk was beginning to fall and the temperature had dropped to a mellow warmth. Jasper could smell the cooked chicken and was slavering in an alarming fashion so I gave him a generous portion in his own dish and then set about unpacking my shopping.

From Hubert's fridge I'd acquired cheese, some bacon and half a dozen eggs. I put together a chicken salad and washed it down with the red wine, which was barely palatable but the more I drank of it the more I liked it. I then made coffee, ate the cream doughnut and gave Jasper a plain biscuit, explaining to him that cream doughnuts were most unhealthy, especially for dogs. I don't think he was convinced.

After our meal I made up the bed, had a shower in the space that was no bigger than one of Hubert's coffins and got so claustrophobic that I made my escape after a very perfunctory dousing. Then I lay curled up with Jasper on the thin mattress of my bed and stared up at the caravan ceiling, which appeared black in the light of the paraffin lamp. It took a few moments for me to realize that the ceiling wasn't black with dirt, it was black with thousands of tiny insects. I quickly pulled the sheet over my head and although I thought I ought to be concerned about my 'plague' I fell asleep easily. Only to be woken soon after by my mobile phone. I answered it, thick-voiced, under the bed-clothes.

Two

It was of course Hubert. The gist of his call was that if I were feeling lonely he would come for the day.

'I'm fine, thanks,' I said in reply.

'The weather's on the change,' he said dolefully.

'I'll cope.'

'How's Jasper?'

I had a feeling that was the real reason for his call. 'Jasper,' I said, 'is in doggie paradise.' I told him I was exploring the delights of Llandudno in the morning and with a 'Cheerio then – take care,' the conversation was at an end.

The following morning the weather was 'on the turn'. It was mild but it was no longer high summer. It was more mellow autumn but at least it was dry and after a prolonged breakfast and a short walk it was about eleven when I began the drive into Llandudno. Parking was a problem but eventually I managed to find a place in a side street some way from the sea. Jasper, fired with enthusiasm by the smell of the sea air, was highly excited. I was less so. I was easily the youngest person there. Perhaps it was the week of a pensioners' convention I thought. Arm in arm they strolled slowly or they sat looking out to sea. Many walked with sticks and I spent some time sitting on a wall playing 'I spy someone under forty'.

For Jasper the call of the sea was too much and he began pulling at the lead, so we made our way to the beach, where I released him and he darted off to the water's edge. I was about to sit down on the sand when I heard someone yelling 'Kate – Kate!' I didn't take any notice. After all, Kate is not an un-common name. But when the yell changed to 'Kate Kinsella – I know it's you,' I had to respond. I turned round and coming to-wards me was a thin woman in her thirties with a camera slung round her neck wearing white shorts and striped socks to match her multi-coloured top. She had long fairish hair and wore sunglasses. She slipped off her glasses as she came closer and she was smiling broadly. Her eyes were a clear blue, her eyelashes well loaded with mascara. There was only one problem. I didn't know her from Adam, Eve or anyone else – she was a total stranger.

'Kate – I can't believe it. Fancy seeing you here.'

My embarrassment was total. Who the hell was she? 'Hi,' I said brightly, trying to stave

23

off the moment when I had to admit I didn't know her.

'It's been years,' she said. I crossed my fingers hoping desperately she wouldn't ask how many.

'If you're not busy,' she said, 'how about a coffee?'

I struggled for an excuse. 'I can't really. I've got my dog with me.' I pointed out from the beach to where Jasper was chasing a blue ball that bobbed about in the water. 'Jasper!' I called and he came running to examine my new companion. As promiscuous as ever he fawned and then rolled on his back hoping no doubt she would tickle his tum. She didn't. She merely said, 'Outside cafés don't mind dogs. Come on, Kate. There's one across the road with seats outside.'

It was a self-service place – all the customers, bar us, being middle-aged or elderly and mostly female – but I warmed to her and the venue when she returned to the table with coffee and two scones thickly wedged with jam and cream. Not that a coffee and a scone would help me remember who she was. She hadn't been a client. Of that I was sure. Had I met her on holiday or in New Zealand?

'You haven't changed a bit, Kate,' she said, as she raised her coffee cup to her lips. I began eating my scone very slowly, reasoning that if I kept my mouth full I wouldn't have to say much. 'Did you go into nursing?' she asked. I nodded. If we were going that far back there was only one place we could have met – school. So why couldn't I remember her? She obviously hadn't been a particular friend of mine otherwise surely I would have remembered her. Strong doubts about my mental health surfaced and I began to feel even more hot and bothered. I decided to risk it. 'You've changed,' I said. She smiled, revealing neat, even white teeth. And then it clicked – Helen Woods – always at the orthodontist. The same Helen whose socks were whiter than anyone else and who never ate sweets. A real swot too. She wasn't the most popular girl in school but I could remember now she'd wanted to go into politics so we'd presumed she liked being unpopular. From a gangly, toothy schoolgirl she'd turned into an attractive slim woman – what did that say about me who hadn't 'changed a bit'?

I relaxed now that I'd remembered her and we chatted a bit about our school days but strangely we didn't seem to remember things in quite the same way. The present seemed a safer option. 'Are you still nursing?' she asked.

'I'm a private investigator.'

'Wow. That sounds interesting.'

'It can be. And you?'

'I'm a freelance photographer. That's why I'm in Wales – doing some shots for the

Welsh Tourist Board.'

'That sounds interesting,' I said politely. Jasper, who'd been angelic up to now, for some reason started licking at my ankle. I tried to ignore him and think of something intelligent to ask about photography. Nothing sprang to mind so I sipped at my coffee.

'Are you living with anyone?' she asked.

'No. I sort of live alone. I haven't had much luck with men.'

'I didn't until a few months ago. Then I met Paul.' She smiled with such happiness that I knew that I was in for a longish session about how wonderful he was. I suppose it's something every single dreads because it throws up all the sort of questions you want to avoid – 'What's she got that I haven't got?' being the most usual, although in this case it was fairly obvious.

I listened while she told me about her last photo assignment in India and how she'd literally bumped into him in a local camera shop. He was tall dark and handsome and, it seemed, rich. He would be, wouldn't he! Anyone I bump into is either drunk, smelly or totally obnoxious. Anyway Paul was the personification of perfect manhood. He worked as a financial advisor, was an artist in his spare time, specializing in watercolours, lived in a house by the sea in Cornwall and was a widower. They were planning their wedding for late September.

'You will come won't you, Kate?' asked Helen earnestly.

'I'll try.'

'Perhaps you could come and stay with us before then.'

This threw me somewhat. I hardly knew her. 'My mother is getting on a bit – she ... gets a bit forgetful,' I muttered by way of an excuse.

Helen raised her eyebrows slightly, no doubt guessing I'd improvised.

'How's *your* mum?' I asked.

'She died. Two years ago – cancer.'

'I'm sorry.'

Helen gave a little shrug of her shoulders. 'I miss her so much, especially with my wedding coming up. And I haven't made many friends of my own in Cornwall – I don't know why.'

'It's being self-employed. It's a lonely existence.'

She smiled briefly. 'Is that it? I was beginning to think it was me.'

We chatted about India for a while, finished eating and drinking and I was raring to go. Helen was nice enough but a little serious and earnest. She wasn't the sort to go clubbing with or even have a girlie night in with. And worse, there was something – needy – about her. I couldn't quite put my finger on why I felt that. After all, she was in love and presumably he was her 'rock'.

I was about to use Jasper's toilet needs as an excuse when she said, 'Do you deal with any unusual cases, Kate?'

'In their own way I suppose they are all a bit unusual. If it starts out as a relatively normal investigation, that state doesn't last long. I'm not the world's best private 'tec.'

'Have you ever dealt with ... ghosts?'

I laughed. 'That's for exorcists and I don't believe in ghosts.'

'I do.'

I shrugged. 'Any reason?'

'I think Paul's house is haunted.'

'There is an answer to that,' I said, not wanting to get embroiled in any super-natural mumbo-jumbo.

'What's that?'

'Sell up and move to somewhere that isn't haunted.'

She wasn't peeved at my bluntness. 'We would,' she said, 'but no one wants to buy it.'

'Why not?'

'It's isolated and fairly near the edge of the cliff...' She paused and I knew that another ghost reference wasn't far off. 'I think prospective buyers also think it's haunted.'

'Why would they think that?'

'They sense it.'

'Sense what? How does this ... haunting manifest itself?'

'It's nothing tangible, at least not to viewers or even to Paul.'

'So why is the house affecting you?'

'It's got a history.'

'Is it that old?'

'No, I mean a recent history.'

'Which is?'

Helen looked out towards the sea. 'It's a very sad story ... Paul's wife committed suicide and killed their two children.'

'Oh,' I said, shocked. 'That's tragic. Did it happen in the house?'

She shook her head. 'Not exactly but near the house. She drugged the children and herself and then walked them over the cliff edge. Paul was devastated. He was asleep in the house. He woke up and went out looking for them and saw them all smashed up on the rocks.'

'That's not something you get over easily.'

'He says at first he was in shock, then he was angry and wanted to sell up and live abroad but no one wanted to buy the house and he was too depressed to put in any effort so he stayed on.'

'But the house affects you?'

'I don't sleep very well. I hear things. It's got to the point where I'm frightened to go to bed at night. Sometimes it's footsteps. Sometimes I think I hear the children crying.'

'That's horrible,' I said. 'But do you think you're just dwelling on what happened? Stress and imagination can play tricks with your hearing.'

'Do you think that's what it is?' I could see Helen was clutching at my straw of comfort.

I nodded. 'Perhaps you need to move out for a while, at least until the stress of the wedding is over.'

'I've thought about that and talked to Paul about it but he doesn't want me to do that and says that I'm being – hypersensitive...' She paused and looked at me earnestly. 'You don't think I've got psychic powers do you?'

'I doubt that. I'm a psychic sceptic and I don't think you should go down that road.'

Jasper woke from his nap and wagged his tail at me in anticipation of either a walk or a titbit. My scone was long forgotten and I hadn't left a crumb. I noticed now that Helen had left half of hers. That's how slim people do it I thought. They have that clever knack of not clearing their plate. So simple, but so hard to do when every day as a child you were encouraged to eat more and a clear plate was rewarded with a round of applause. If not, you had the additional worry of the starving children in Africa, who most certainly wouldn't leave anything on their plates. Helen's family had been well off, so I supposed her mother didn't worry about food left on the plate.

'I've got to go, Kate. I'm going to Rhyl now before it gets dark.' She leant forward and her blue eyes were bright and eager. 'I want your business card,' she said. She handed me hers and I rummaged in my purse for one of mine. It had a slightly chewed appearance and as I certainly didn't want her as a client I hoped it would show I wasn't the dynamic type. She looked at it and murmured, 'Fancy you becoming a private investigator.'

'There you go,' I said. 'I earn a living.'

'I expect you meet some interesting people,' she said. I smiled but thought to myself they were only 'interesting' in the deranged, damaged and desperate categories. I'd faced the fact some time ago that 'normal' people do not require my services. And I had a nervous inkling that Helen Woods, having found me by chance, wasn't going to let me go.

'You will come and stay,' she said, 'won't you? A long weekend ... soon. Then you can meet Paul.'

I could hardly wait, I thought cynically, but I nodded weakly and smiled.

The drive back to Nefyn was uneventful except for the ominous black clouds that loomed overhead. About an hour after we arrived back at the caravan the storm broke. Jasper and I huddled under the bedclothes as the wind rocked us, the thunder deafened us and the hailstones fell on the metal roof like machine-gun fire. Once when I peeked out between thunderclaps I actually saw the forked lightning through the curtains and

I'm not sure who was more scared, Jasper or me. He was shaking more but I was most definitely unnerved. Eventually the storm passed over leaving only the clatter of torrential rain and puddles outside the caravan as big as ponds. 'Don't you worry, Jasper,' I whispered in his ear as I cuddled him to me. 'Tomorrow we're going home.'

Three

Arriving back at Humberstone's I knew something was wrong when I saw a little group of staff standing around a hearse. They looked far more sombre than usual. I parked my car and watched as one of the pallbearers reverently carried a tiny coffin into the chapel of rest followed by the rest of the staff. I was slightly worried because Hubert wasn't at the forefront carrying the coffin.

I rushed straight up to Hubert's flat. He wasn't in the sitting room or the kitchen. I guessed he was in his office so I thought it best to wait for him. I try to avoid too much involvement with 'downstairs'. I've never wanted to be involved in the funeral business and yet sometimes I feel that Hubert would love me to be the heir to his kingdom.

I was about to feed Jasper when he began to get agitated. I opened the kitchen door and he ran along the hallway to my office and began barking excitedly at the door. I followed, opened the door and there was Hubert sat at my desk head in hands. He

33

quickly tried to compose himself but it was obvious he'd been crying. 'What's happened?' I asked, moving towards him and then putting my arms around him. I'd never seen Hubert cry before and like the storm it unnerved me. I was obviously squeezing him a bit hard in my anxiety.

'You'll have to let go, Kate. I can't breathe.'

'I'll get you a brandy,' I said.

'OK. But stop fussing. I'm fine now.' He didn't look fine to me. His eyes were reddened blobs, his cheeks ashen.

The brandy, a treble, though he didn't seem to notice or care, brought some colour to his face. 'Sorry, Kate. This one just got to me.'

The small coffin I had seen contained the body of a three-year-old boy, starved and beaten to death by his stepfather. 'I've never seen anything so tragic,' said Hubert, his eyes filling with tears. 'Little lad had legs like matchsticks. He was all covered in bruises and burns. And he had the face of an angel.'

I couldn't think of anything to say so I murmured that he would never suffer again. Hubert's shoulders stiffened. 'I'd like to kill the bastard who could do that to a little child.'

'Is he in prison?'

'Yes. And his so-called mother.'

We sat in silence for a few moments. There seemed to be nothing we could say.

'Will you do me a favour, Kate?'

I hesitated but only for a moment. 'Of course. What is it?'

'Attend his funeral. It seems only his grandparents are coming. I've seen it before when children are murdered by their parents – no one wants to attend the funeral. Condemned by association I suppose. The shame of it all – it's all a bloody shame.'

'Of course I'll come if that's what you want. When is it?'

'Tomorrow.'

I'd never attended a child's funeral before although a friend of mine had quit her job as a children's ward sister because she had 'attended one funeral too many'. I dreaded it and that night in restless sleep I dreamt my mother was in sole charge of Megan's Katy and whilst she was happily swigging vodka Katy was happily playing with matches. I woke at dawn, felt exhausted and dreaded the day ahead.

The funeral was at eleven and by eight a.m. I was dressed and ready and unable to concentrate on anything else. The grandparents had left the choice of clergy to Hubert, stipulating only that the funeral should not be too religious.

When my phone rang at nine thirty I felt inclined to ignore it but it provided a diversion from waiting so I answered it. 'Hello, Kate,' said the voice. I recognized her *now*. It was Helen. 'It was so lovely to meet up with you again,' she said. 'I just had to ring you and invite you properly to Tamberlake – that's the name of the house.' I was lost for words. 'That's very nice of you,' I managed. Silence – an awkward silence.

'What about the week after next? Paul's away for a few days but you could stay on and meet him.'

A few days! 'I really am very busy, Helen.' Silence again.

'Please, Kate. I'm scared to be alone. Please. I'll pay for your time.'

That made me feel even worse. 'There's no need for that. I'll do it for old times' sake. I'll stay until Paul comes back.'

'Thank you, Kate – thank you. You really are an angel. He's leaving on Saturday. Could you come in time for lunch?'

By now I was past worrying about the day or the time. 'Fine,' I said. 'I'll be there about two.' She gave me the address and thanked me profusely again so that I felt quite churlish. Most people, I thought, would love a few days in Cornwall in the summer. I was behaving as if it was a chore.

When I told Hubert about my trip he didn't look too pleased. When I mentioned my nervous host and ghosts he looked even less pleased. 'Don't you believe in ghosts then, Hubert?' I said partly to wind him up because I felt sure he didn't.

'I wish I did,' he said glumly. 'Then murderous bastards who abuse children would be haunted until the day they died. Life isn't fair though is it? They have no conscience or they wouldn't do it. Seeing ghosts needs sensitivity and imagination – that's all it is – a vivid imagination or wishful thinking.'

I didn't quite understand what he was getting at. 'You mean you have to *want* to see a ghost before one will pop up?'

He shrugged. Maybe he wasn't sure what he meant either.

The next hour dragged by. I walked Jasper while Hubert drank coffee and read the paper. Then I sat in my office and scanned my e-mail 'spam'. I'm surprised junk e-mail isn't called 'scam' because that's what they are. They feed on universal anxiety – debt, obesity and sex. *In debt? Settle your debts now! Weight loss? Lose 30 lbs in a month! Penis too small? You can be extended!* Sometimes they play on sheer curiosity to get you to open the stupid things – *Hi! I've been looking for you!* I deleted my eight 'messages' without opening them and wondered if it would be worth my while to advertise myself on the Internet. How would I word mine? *Hi! Is your husband having an affair?* Or *Police too busy to help? You need an expert.* That was pushing it a bit but I could try. Maybe *Missing loved one? Make the search ours.* I quite liked that and decided to discuss it with Hubert after the funeral.

Just before ten forty-five I was ushered by Hubert to the waiting Daimler – one of two that would follow the hearse. The sun was shining, inappropriately I thought. Funerals belonged in the rain and the cold. It was ten stately minutes to the cemetery and the car's quiet dark interior gave me the chance to think about Darren – murdered brutally in his fourth year. He wasn't the only one of course. A child who'd been given the short straw in life. There were no excuses. Had he ever known any happiness I wondered. I was grateful when my short but lonely journey was over.

The officiating vicar stood at the door of the chapel to meet the maternal grand-parents. On the tiny coffin had been placed a floral teddy bear. The grandmother was already sobbing and the vicar put her arms around her and hugged her tight. The Rev. Anne White was in her forties with short fair hair and the look of a kindly headmistress. She shook my hand and thanked me for coming and then as I walked into the chapel and saw the coffin, so small and surrounded by flowers, a lump caught in my throat and stayed there.

'Think of Darren,' said the vicar, 'as a tiny seedling of God, cruelly cut down before he had time to grow. He knew the love of grandparents and he had some happy times. He will always live in their hearts and now he also lives safe in the arms of Jesus.' She followed this with a special prayer for children but by then I was only aware of the tears coursing down my face.

As the coffin was carried out a medley of children's songs were relayed throughout the empty chapel. 'The Wheels on the Bus go Round and Round', and 'Incey Wincey Spider'. We walked out of the chapel and into the sunshine to the sound of 'Jingle Bells'.

After the interment Hubert told me we would be going to the catering suite at Humberstone's. Hubert travelled with me this time. I'd rather hoped we could go straight to a local hostelry. He didn't say much on the journey. Just that he was glad it was over. But it wasn't over of course. The 'refreshments' had to be endured.

Hubert sat me at one of the tables, bistro-style in pink and grey, with the grandparents Alan and Jackie. They were in their late forties, their faces ravaged with tears. Hubert brought a trolley of drinks so that we could help ourselves. We all chose brandy – neat. 'I blame myself,' said Jackie, her voice thick with emotion. 'We should have stopped her seeing that ... monster. He's ruined all our lives. Darren was a lovely kid, so happy until *he* came into their lives. Six months with *him* and he'd killed our Darren.'

'It wasn't our fault, love,' said Alan, putting

his arm round his wife. 'We warned her that he was the jealous type. We told her some men couldn't stand the reminder of another man. She wouldn't listen.'

'And now she's barely twenty and in prison.'

'Maybe she'll learn some sense and stop taking drugs. It was *him* that started her on them.'

Jackie nodded miserably and sipped at her brandy. Then she seemed to notice me for the first time. 'You're Kate aren't you?' I nodded. 'Do thank your husband for us won't you? It was ever so kind of him to pay for everything and it was such a lovely service. I keep thinking of what that vicar said. "Safe in the arms of Jesus." That comforts me.'

I blinked back a tear. This was not the time to deny Hubert being my husband.

He must have known I was gunning for him, because he disappeared as soon as Alan and Jackie left. No one had eaten any of the sandwiches but I'd sunk a few brandies and all I could do now was lie down in a darkened room and think of anything but Darren. What did spring to mind though was the tragedy of Helen's fiancé Paul. He'd lost a wife and two children and by the wife's own hand. Of course the question remained – why? I supposed that suicides where no explanatory note is left meant the grieving

40

relatives foundered in guilt, secrecy and ignorance. Was it their fault? Why hadn't they noticed their loved one had lost the will to live? Death by suicide seemed to me a punishment for those left behind. I'd experienced the death of someone I loved but it was a freak accident and it was a consolation to know he'd died so suddenly and swiftly.

Later in the afternoon I met up with Hubert in the kitchen. He had Jasper under one arm and was back to his usual self so I said nothing about being accused of being his wife. He would be embarrassed and so would I. Plus it might upset Jasper. Instead I mentioned my forthcoming trip to Cornwall.

'I could do with a break,' he said.

'This is more baby-sitting an ex-school friend.' He was busy making tea so he didn't answer and I was still thinking about Paul's wife. 'You've had experience of suicides,' I said. 'What's your opinion?'

He gave me a piercing look. 'Well it's an option. And bloody selfish.'

'Yes but sometimes it seems to happen for no apparent reason.'

Hubert set down cups and saucers. 'Misery is the reason, hopelessness. A view of the world where it's black as night and the sun don't rise.'

'You sound as if you've been there?'

'I have, Kate,' he said edgily, 'but I don't

41

want to talk about it.' There was quite a bit I didn't know about Hubert's past but what did it matter? From Hubert's anecdotes and observing his staff they seemed a cheerful bunch, not as prone to suicide as farmers. Strange that those surrounded by death seemed happier than those who provided our food. But perhaps such close contact with death removed all the fear.

'Surely,' I said, warming to the subject, 'if people acknowledged they were miserable and depressed and sought help, at least there would be less unexplained suicides.'

'Well,' said Hubert as he poured the tea. 'I reckon depression is the new leprosy.'

'What do you mean?'

'I mean people will be kind for a while and then when you don't "cheer up" they avoid you. Misery is catching. The world is difficult enough and some people cope better than others do. But the old adage is still true, "Laugh and the world laughs with you – cry and you cry alone." '

I knew that to be true. If I ever found a boyfriend who could cope with tears I reckon I'd be in love. Most men I know don't realize that a cuddle is worth a thousand words. They don't have to solve your problems, just be gently physical. But then, as Hubert contends, if depression is contagious its not surprising men get a slightly sick expression when their woman feels low.

'By the way,' said Hubert. 'You did really well with that couple.'

'I didn't say a word.'

'You listened. That's all that mattered.' He looked at me quizzically.

'Don't look at me like that, Hubert. The funeral business is *not* my forte.'

'Well,' he muttered. 'Tell me something that is.'

'Ghost-busting?'

'Very funny. If you bust a ghost make sure you get well paid for it.'

'I'm not doing it for the money.'

'Well what are you doing it for?'

'Old times' sake.'

He raised an eyebrow. I kept quiet then. Because I still had only the vaguest memories of Helen Woods. And I had the feeling that it would be better to leave it that way.

Four

Finding Cornwall took hours but at least I couldn't miss it. Finding Tamberlake was a different matter – three random stops to ask people I was so sure were locals resulted in apologies for their only being on holiday. I began to suspect that the native Cornish hibernated in the peak holiday season and who could blame them? Eventually I stopped at an estate agent in the small town of Trevelly. A fresh-faced young man looked me up and down as if assessing whether I could afford a wooden shed in Cornwall. By his expression he guessed I couldn't. But at least he'd heard of Tamberlake and he gave me good directions although his three miles were 'country' miles and I would have guessed at six miles at the very least. The last mile always seems the longest and this mile down a narrow unmade road was no exception. High hedges occluded any view but through my open car window I could smell the sea.

The house, when I saw it between the long grass and the trees that surrounded it, was

44

an ivy-clad Victorian monstrosity with port-holes, peeling paint and an air of sad defeat. I hoped the need for a 'makeover' was only on the outside. Helen must have seen my arrival, for before I could use the brass knocker she had opened the door. She wore jeans and a white blouse tied at the front to expose her neat midriff. 'I'm so glad to see you, Kate,' she said earnestly. 'Paul had to leave yesterday and one night on my own was enough. I haven't slept.' She grabbed my travel bag and took my arm gently but I felt as if I was being dragged in.

As I glimpsed the hall I wasn't surprised she thought the place was haunted. It was gloomy and smelt of damp. Perhaps, I thought, the floral décor was trying to make a statement but I couldn't quite work out what it was. 'Wonderful isn't it?' said Helen. I supposed she was looking for reassurance so I mumbled about character and atmosphere.

'How many rooms does it have?' I asked.

'Six bedrooms, two bathrooms, three reception rooms, kitchen of course, attic and cellar. We use the cellar for Paul's huge wine collection. Come on, I'll show you round.'

'Would you mind if I had a coffee first?'

'Of course, sorry, Kate. You must be tired. Of course, we'll have lunch and do the grand tour afterwards.' That sounded good to me and we made our way below-stairs to the kitchen, which boasted a pine table that would seat eight. The Aga sat like a culinary Buddha on one wall and the sink appeared to be the original butler sink but at least with the addition of a hot tap. There was a small barred window that looked out towards an overgrown lawn and it was the sort of kitchen that needed lights on night and day. Two light bulbs covered in lampshades made of beige Bakelite lit the room but only in patches. There were several shadowy corners. 'We do have a pantry,' said Helen excitedly and showed me to a door of the walk-in pantry. It contained mostly empty pickling bottles. 'I haven't quite got round to home-made jam and pickles yet.'

'Not to worry,' I said with a nervous laugh. 'I've been pickled myself but I prefer a supermarket to do the hard graft.' She smiled as if she thought she ought to and then said, 'Paul loves all the old traditional ways.'

'Well let him do the pickling then.'

She looked at me as if I'd blasphemed, quickly composed herself and managed a tight smile. 'Come on, let's sit down. Lunch is all ready.'

Lunch was a prawn and fresh crab salad with white crusty bread. 'This bread is delicious,' I said between hungry mouthfuls, although I did slow down when I saw Helen was pushing her food around the plate.

'I made it myself. I thought it was pretty good.'

'Clever you,' I said. 'It really is the best home-made bread I've ever tasted.' Helen smiled cheerfully, her equilibrium restored. We had strawberries and cream to follow and I offered to wash up but she opened a cupboard door and there sat a dishwasher. I was impressed with the disguise – the twenty-first century had come to Tamberlake.

There followed the grand tour of the house. The sitting room had William Morris wallpaper and original watercolours on the walls, mostly of Cornwall, and the flat-screen, multi-channel TV was encased in a double-door reproduction 'antique'.

Eventually I was shown my room and it was a relief when she said, 'You get un-packed and have a rest. I've got things to do so just relax and come down when you're ready. Supper is at seven thirty – it'll be a bit basic.'

When she'd gone I sat on the double bed and gazed at the ornate cornices, the heavy floor-to-ceiling drapes – floral of course, and with tassels – and thought that the stream-lined Helen belonged not here but in some white minimalist apartment in London. I unpacked, noted I had my own TV and desk, a bowl of fruit on my bedside table alongside a cerise lamp and a selection of new paperback books. A box of chocs and a bathroom en suite and I would have been quite content. To check out if it felt haunted I walked round the room to find any cold spots and couldn't find one. I wasn't surprised of course.

A bit gloomy the house might be but I got no impression of any ghosties being likely. Although I had to admit it was far too large for one person and I would have felt uneasy being there on my own. The 'tour' hadn't included all the rooms and the attic and cellar remained unseen. One thing had struck me. There seemed to be no evidence of children ever having been in the house. There were no photographs of either his wife or children on display but, with a wife in waiting, perhaps he thought it politic to keep them out of view.

I lay back against the patchwork quilt which ill matched the rest of the room and, promising myself a quick nap, I closed my eyes. When I woke, Helen was knocking at my door telling me it was after seven. She now wore a long black skirt and a white lacy top. I felt grubby but she said the meal was ready so we may as well eat.

If only all my meals were so 'basic'. We sat in the kitchen eating crispy duck breast with red wine, new potatoes and green beans with anchovies. Helen had as much on her plate as mine but she ate only a quarter and I, of course, polished off every last morsel. Although the food was delicious the conversation was stilted and awkward, but the accompanying fine red wine soon had Helen talking about photography. Not a subject I knew much about because if I was going anywhere it was the camera I usually forgot. Over apple crumble and clotted cream I asked about Paul's job.

'It's been a bit hectic for him lately,' she said. 'A few years back he was a corporate financial advisor but he didn't feel they paid him enough so he's been freelance for the last eighteen months. I think he made a hasty decision after his wife...'

'Does it upset you to talk about it?'

She stroked the side of her face thoughtfully. 'Yes I suppose it does. I love Paul to bits but we never mention the past. He says the past is best forgotten and he has enough painful anniversaries to cope with anyway.'

'And you met him by chance?'

'Yes, in a camera shop. Life is really weird isn't it? We got chatting as we waited in the queue and he asked me to go for a coffee with him.'

The wine – we were now on a dessert wine – had gone to my head and I related to her one or two 'pick-ups' of mine that had no such happy endings. I'd bumped into a really good-looking guy in a supermarket. He'd taken me for a coffee. Three coffees later he was still chuntering about the futures market. He could have been talking in Mandarin Chinese, because I didn't have a clue what he was talking about. Every time I opened my mouth he talked even faster. In the end I gave up.

Helen had had similar experiences but hers were more the sudden lunge that came out of the blue. Paul, in contrast, made no unexpected lunges, had courted her with flowers and chocolates and letting her see his wine cellar.

As Helen made coffee I wondered why she had chosen me to keep her company. I didn't think it was because she liked me. The more I dredged my schoolgirl memories the more I realized, apart from the fact her socks were whiter than white and that she wore braces on her teeth, we'd had very little contact. She'd had, I remembered, a best friend called Gill who had a high-pitched laugh and a tendency to practical jokes.

'What happened to Gill?' I asked as she handed me a cup of proper coffee.

'We've seen each other a bit over the years. She's met Paul...' She broke off. 'To be honest they didn't get on. He thought she was nosy and flighty.'

'Is she coming to the wedding?'

'I think so.' She sounded unsure and a bit nervous.

'I'm surprised you haven't several friends

who would give their eye teeth for a freebie in Cornwall.'

'I wanted you.'

'Because I'm a private detective?'

'Not exactly.'

'Why then?'

She shrugged. 'I suppose it's because you're so down to earth. You don't believe in ghosts. You see, I think Gill *does* believe in ghosts. She would turn me into a nervous wreck.'

I sipped at my coffee. 'When Paul is here have you ever been ... nervous?'

'Once or twice but he soon calms me down.'

'Does he want to sell up and move?'

'Oh yes. This was his childhood home and it costs a fortune to keep it going. He's keen to find somewhere more modern and with less land to worry about. Three acres of land takes a lot of looking after. And it's got its own patch of private beach. I'll take you down there tomorrow. It's beautiful.'

Helen seemed reluctant to leave the kitchen and insisted that she needed no help clearing up. She guided me to the sitting room and exposed the TV screen. It was growing dark by now so she pulled the drapes and switched on lamps and left me sitting in a high-backed armchair with my feet on a footstool. I felt like grandma. All I needed was a rug over my knees.

Now that darkness had fallen the room seemed full of shadows. Behind me a standard lamp with gold tassels cast a fairly dim light and I half expected a maid to arrive saying she'd turned down my bed. I flicked the TV on and turned down the volume. I couldn't hear anything specific, no creaking boards, no running water, certainly no footsteps or voices. I could hear a slight rustle of the trees outside and wondered if a Cornish storm was brewing. There was certainly nothing that disturbed me unduly ... except one thing. How had the children found this rambling gloomy house? Was the house itself the cause of Paul's wife becoming so deranged?

I switched up the volume on the remote and tried to relax in my granny chair. It was none of my business after all. I was simply spending a few days keeping an old friend company. Except that she wasn't an old friend and maybe I'm acquiring a more detective-like suspicious nature. Hubert would say, 'About bloody time.' He accuses me of being too trusting but this time I did feel there was a hidden agenda, but as yet I didn't know what it was.

Helen came back after half an hour or so and sat beside me in a matching chair. 'Paul rang. I told him my ex-nurse friend had arrived so that pleased him.'

'You didn't tell him I was a private detective?'

'No.'

'Why not?'

She avoided my eyes. 'It didn't seem important.'

I stared at her pointedly and eventually she looked at me. 'Do you think he's seeing someone else?' I asked.

Her response was shocked and immediate. 'No I do not! That's a horrible thing to say. We're getting married in a few weeks.'

'Precisely,' I said. 'So you want to be sure?'

'I am sure. Since his wife died I'm the first woman he's been involved with. He is not a womanizer...' She broke off. 'Honestly, Kate. I don't have any suspicions like that.'

'What suspicions do you have?'

'None at all. It's just my nerves. This house. Its history. It's getting to me. Paul is the one stable focus of my life.'

Her voice was wavering now as if on the edge of tears and I felt guilty for upsetting her. After all, she was a great hostess, I was well fed and watered and I was casting aspersions on her beloved. I mentally slapped my wrist and said, 'Of course he is. I'm sorry.'

'I didn't mean to get snappy,' she said. 'Would you like to see a photo of him?'

'Of course. Then I'll know who we're talking about.'

From a walnut dresser she produced two photos. Handing me the first she said, 'I didn't take this one.'

I studied it closely. Only one word came to mind. 'Wow!' I breathed. No wonder she was in love with him. He was sitting on a black stallion, wearing a tight white tee shirt, black jodhpurs and boots. He had a polo stick in his hand. Tanned, handsome and muscular – he was the stuff dreams are made of.

'And this is the one I took,' she said, handing me the second one. This showed the symmetry of his face; his dark sexy eyes all enhanced by a dark suit and a white shirt. No wonder he didn't make pickles. He wasn't the type. A man like that doesn't wear a pinny. 'Polo's an expensive sport,' I said casually.

'He plays with a friend but only when he's abroad.'

'Where is he now?'

'Argentina.'

We fell silent then. He may not be a womanizer, I thought, but any woman I knew would be more than happy to polish his polo stick.

That night I woke up twice, not because of any ghostly happenings, but because of erotic dreams of handsome polo players. They were the best dreams I'd had in ages.

At breakfast Helen looked tired. 'I had a lousy night,' she said. 'Did you hear anything?'

'Not a thing.'

'I didn't either,' she answered, but I knew by the anxious expression in her eyes she was lying. I didn't pursue it, because there was nothing I could do to alter her state of mind except be around until the gorgeous hunk returned.

'I've made us a picnic,' she said, opening the pantry door and producing a large picnic basket.

'You must have been up at the crack of dawn.'

'I never sleep beyond six,' she said. 'In fact I hardly sleep much at all.'

By ten we left to go down to the beach. I carried the basket and Helen held back the brambles and tall fronds of greenery along the narrow path. Still I hadn't seen the sea but I could smell it. Occasionally a slight breeze rustled the dry grasses and bushes and as we rounded a slight bend there was a break in the vegetation and in front of us was a vast expanse of sea. No ripples, just a glassy turquoise plate. 'It's so beautiful,' I said.

'Yes,' she said. 'This is the path his wife took. And the children of course. Going to their deaths.'

Five

Another night had passed during which I'd slept like a drunken slug. I actually felt guilty that I was sleeping so well, because Helen looked pale and exhausted. I offered to cook all the meals and help with the housework but she said she liked to keep busy. Presuming, I suppose, that I didn't. Actually I was beginning to get a little bored. During the morning I decided to take a walk down the path to the beach.

The sun shone warmly making a snug bower of the path. Two butterflies led my walk, a bee buzzed and a kestrel flew high above. As I walked I soon lost interest in the flora and fauna for two little niggles crept into my mind. The first was that not once had Helen mentioned Paul's wife's name, nor those of the children. Did that make them seem less real to her or did saying their names upset her? I didn't *need* to know their names of course. It was merely curiosity but it struck me as odd. My second niggle was, on that fateful night whilst Paul slept, was his wife carrying a torch, because unless there was a full moon she would have been walking blind.

The path dipped down quite steeply to the beach but it wasn't dangerous. Further along through yellowing grass was the cliff edge itself. I abandoned the beach path and walked towards the edge of the cliff. It was hard to miss in daylight even though there were no warning signs. At night, though, it would have been impossible to see. Going over the edge would have been easy. Easy enough to fall accidentally. I stood well back and looked down. From that angle I could see only jagged rocks.

I rejoined the path to the beach and once there I sat for a while in solitary splendour, staring out to sea and listening to the gentle swish of the sea against the sand. I would have liked a paddle but that involved sand between the toes and I hadn't brought a towel with me.

Arriving back at the house I found Helen in the kitchen slaving over a meat pie. Personally I thought she was taking the domestic goddess thing a bit far but I could eat whatever she could cook so I wasn't going to complain. She looked a better colour now but the kitchen was incredibly warm and full of the smell of fresh-baked bread. 'Guess what?' she said excitedly. I thought that maybe Paul was on his way home just as I was getting used to real home cooking. 'Gill's coming. Isn't that wonderful?'

'Why the change of heart?'

'She heard you were here and she more or less invited herself.'

'What about Paul?'

'You won't tell him will you?' Again there was that note of anxiety in her voice. Was she afraid of losing him, I wondered, or just afraid of him.

'I won't be seeing him will I?'

'Maybe not until the wedding. You will come won't you?'

'Yes. If you want me to.'

She rested her floury hands on the wooden board in front of her as though she needed support and a few seconds later her face drained of colour. 'I feel a bit dizzy,' she muttered.

I insisted she had a proper rest on her bed and I took her up to the master bedroom and helped her on to the bed. I closed the curtains and crept out of the room. I wasn't sure what was wrong with her but I wasn't going to panic yet. She'd mumbled something about Gill arriving late afternoon and that the pie was for supper.

I went back to the kitchen, tidied up and emptied the dishwasher and then with nothing else in mind I decided to explore the rest of the house. I hadn't yet seen the attic room or the cellar. The attic was up a narrow winding staircase and at the top I was surprised to find it was locked. I was both disappointed and intrigued but I went back to the floor below and quietly opened the remaining three bedroom doors. One room was obviously a guest room. The other two were empty. The two empty rooms had been redecorated with fresh white paintwork and a rose-trellis wallpaper. The wallpaper looked expensive and surely only a man could decide to have two rooms identically decorated. Had he over-ordered on the rolls of wallpaper or had he done it in a hurry for some reason? I was obviously beginning to get paranoid because I kept fretting over such trivialities. What was there to worry about after all? I wasn't marrying him, although remembering what a hunk he was perhaps I was a tad jealous.

Back in my room my mobile phone bleeped at me from the depths of my handbag. I had two unanswered calls, both I presumed from Hubert. As I tapped in his number 'Network Failure' flashed at me.

I rang Hubert from the wall phone in the kitchen. 'I've been worried,' he said. 'What's going on?'

'There's nothing to worry about. I'm just keeping an old school friend company.'

'No ghosties and ghoulies then?'

'I've slept really well, haven't even heard as much as a creaking floorboard.'

'When are you coming back?'

'I'm not sure. Unexpectedly she has a real friend coming down today so I may be surplus to requirements.'

'You've had a few queries,' he said.

'Anything ... interesting?'

'There's a Mafia killing the police are stuck on and they thought you might be able to help with a double shooting at the Fuchsia Society.'

'Very funny, Hubert. I take it that means I've only had the usual crank calls.'

'Not that cranky.'

'David didn't phone?'

'No. Were you expecting him to?'

'It would have been nice.'

'You're not interested in him so why bother?'

'I'm a woman. I'm entitled to be illogical.'

'How's the food?'

'Terrific.'

'See you then ... whenever.'

At one p.m. I peeped in on Helen. She was sound asleep so lunch was a DIY job. I made myself a cheese sandwich and sat in the kitchen reading a novel with a 'feel-good' factor. It was set in Tuscany amongst the olive groves. I skipped the bits about olive-growing and hoped that the love interest would hold me but it didn't and I soon got restless. I missed having Jasper to walk, because a walk with no purpose seems to me to be a waste of time. I wandered the house for a while and was about to view Paul's wine collection in the cellar when I heard a car draw up outside.

Gill, small and bouncy, stepped out of a snappy red convertible. I opened the front door and we stood looking at each other for several seconds, then she hugged me. 'I'm not going to say you haven't changed,' she said. 'You're looking good.'

'So are you,' I said. Her round face and curly dark hair made her look young, twenty-five-ish, and she looked the picture of health. 'I suppose Helen's in the kitchen,' she said, as she lugged a huge holdall through the front door.

'No, she's asleep. She hasn't been sleeping at night.'

'Huh! Who says love made you happy. Load of old tosh. Every time I've been in love I've been as miserable as sin.'

'So you're not married then?'

'Certainly not. I've never found anyone worthy enough. I just have shag buddies – much less trouble.'

Gill as I remembered had always been the outspoken type. She'd been the one to give us our sex education, although to call it 'education' wasn't appropriate. She'd always been a sexual predator and had regaled us virgins with hilarious tales of incompetent boys and ageing would-be sex athletes. Sex

61

was something she didn't take seriously. In fact I didn't think she took life seriously at all and I felt immediately more cheery. I hoped she'd have the same effect on Helen.

I showed Gill to her room. She dropped her holdall in the doorway and cast a dismissive hand over the room. 'This Victoriana crap is awful isn't it? Why try to live in the past? What's wrong with modern stuff? It's no wonder Helen is going off her head.'

'You think she is?'

'Oh yes. I haven't seen her much over the years but she always seemed quite normal until she met him.'

'Why do you think that is?'

Gill dragged her holdall on to the bed. 'She's a typical lovesick woman, seeing booties in the tumble-dryer and an adoring father changing nappies. But Paul isn't the man for that.'

'But he did have children...'

'Those poor little tots,' she said soberly. 'Did anyone ask them what sort of father he was? Or did anyone ask Fran what sort of husband he made?'

'You didn't know her did you?' I asked.

'No ... no I didn't know her. But Helen is a good friend and I may be *persona non grata* with him but I intend to stay in touch with her even if we have to meet secretly.'

I really warmed to Gill then. She was a loyal friend to Helen and my presence didn't

seem necessary at all. Except that I remembered that Helen had said she thought Gill
believed in ghosts. I was about to ask her
about that when she said, 'Come on, let's go
raid the cellar. I could do with a drink.'

I switched on the light at the top of the
stairs and the naked bulb lit the stone steps
downwards. I must have hesitated, because
Gill became impatient. 'I'll go first,' she said.
'I'm used to this dark hole.' I followed her
down and once on the stone floor I was
amazed at the size of it and the fact that
there were two huge barrels on stone plinths
side by side in one corner. The rest of the
cellar contained rack after rack of wine. It
reminded me of a Spanish bodega, cool,
musty and church-like.

'What's in the barrels?' I asked.

'Sherry and brandy I think. Helen says
they've been there for ages.'

'Maturing nicely,' I commented.

Gill laughed. 'Mature and needing the
occasional top-up sounds just like us.'

It was Gill who chose the wine. She picked
a bottle from a section marked 12.

'These are the cheapos. Helen's only allowed these. On special occasions he chooses.
Never pick one of those dusty bottles over
there,' she said, pointing to a section near the
barrels. 'That's the old expensive stuff.
Worth a fortune so I believe.'

The wine may have been a 'cheapo' but I

knew from the label it was over ten pounds a bottle because I'd seen some in our local off-licence. It was good too. Gill declined to eat and we were on our second glass when Helen appeared. Her smile when she saw Gill lit the room. They hugged and then Gill stepped backwards to look properly at Helen. 'You look like shit, Helen. What's wrong with you? You've lost weight and for God's sake you do enough cooking. What do you do with it all? Give it away to the poor of the parish?'

'Stop fussing, Gill. I eat well enough. I'm just not sleeping.'

'Pre-marital nerves?' suggested Gill.

'Of course not. I'm not in the least bit worried about the wedding.'

'It's not the wedding I was thinking of,' said Gill quietly. 'It's the marriage.'

I left them for a while, forced myself to walk the grounds twice and, soon bored, I decided to go to my room to read.

Even lying on the bed I couldn't concentrate on my book. I kept telling myself this whole scenario was nothing to do with me. But I was uneasy and Gill, who seemed so down to earth, had made me think that Helen *was* making a mistake. But then people made poor choices all the time. It wasn't the end of the world. But, of course, it had been for Fran and her children. Had she been in the depths of despair because she too thought the house was haunted or had Paul created her unhappiness? I reasoned that now Gill had arrived I could easily occupy myself finding out more about Fran and the children. If in fact there was anything to find out.

First stop, I thought, would be the local newspaper. Trevelly probably wasn't big enough to have its own newspaper office but Bude or Barnstaple might be. In the morning I'd have a day in town and try to find out a few more details about Fran's death.

I quite dreaded the evening but the meal was good. Helen produced more wine and the time passed, punctuated with giggles and guffaws and a lot of chat about not much in particular. But as the evening wore on Gill became even more talkative, more aggressive. 'Helen,' she said, 'why won't you listen?'

'Because sometimes, Gill, you talk a lot of old cobblers.'

'Would you agree that I've had more experience of men than you?'

Helen nodded reluctantly. It seemed I was to be excluded from this conversation, so I lounged back in the granny chair with my bare feet on a footstool. Outside, it was dark, the wind was whipping up and it had begun to rain heavily. The curtains were still open and I listened to the two of them argue and watched the rain beating against the dormer windows.

'Anyway,' Helen was saying, 'you haven't had a relationship for ages and yet you want me to stay single.'

'That's ridiculous. Of course I want you to have a relationship, but not with Paul. He isn't right for you.'

Gill was on the edge of her chair facing Helen, who sat bolt upright on a low-slung sofa. Helen, I noticed, seemed more spirited since Gill had arrived. She was more sure of herself, more willing to fight her corner. 'Since when have you made a good decision about a man?' asked Helen.

'Since I met Bernard.'

'Who's Bernard?'

'He's someone I've been seeing for the past year. You see, Helen, you don't know every-thing about *me*, your best friend, let alone a man you've only known for a few months.'

Helen seemed a little crushed but she rallied. She'd lost a round but she was still in there.

'And there's your sister,' persisted Gill. 'She doesn't like him does she?'

'My sister doesn't think anyone is good enough for me. I think she's jealous.'

'So everyone is jealous? Even your own sister? Does that make sense?'

'To me it does. You can't deny he's abso-lutely gorgeous.' She turned to me. 'You agree don't you, Kate?' I nodded. Gill sighed loudly.

'I know looks aren't everything but he does make me happy.'

'Does he? I haven't seen that. You've lost weight, you look pale and you're twitchy.'

'I am not twitchy and I'm not going to allow you to upset me.'

Gill looked at me and shrugged her shoulders as if to say – I've tried. But even then she hadn't quite given up. 'What about your career, Helen? You can't make a career out of cooking and cleaning. This house is huge and you do all the cleaning – surely he could afford to employ a cleaner?'

'Of course he can – we've tried but no one wants to work here anymore.'

'What a surprise,' muttered Gill sarcastically.

'As far as my career goes – I don't want to take on long assignments in faraway places. I'm doing shots for the Cornwall Tourist Board and the Wales Tourist Board. I keep busy.'

'That is true,' said Gill with a tight smile.

'Anyway,' said Helen. 'Can we change the subject? There's a favour I want to ask you both.'

'Your wish is our command,' said Gill, still sounding a little sour.

'Will you both come with me to choose my wedding dress?'

Gill didn't answer straight away. 'Yes of course,' she said eventually. 'Just promise me one thing.'

'What's that?'

'No puffed sleeves.'

Helen laughed. 'That deserves a bottle of sparkling wine at the very least. I'll go and get one.'

When she'd gone Gill went to the door to check she was out of earshot before saying, 'She's not that sure. She'd have chosen her dress by now if she was.'

'What is it *exactly* that you have against him?'

She thought for a moment. 'It's a gut feeling, but there is one word I'd use to describe him and that is *sinister*.'

'Why can't Helen see that?' I asked.

'I think she sees that trait in him as being sexy.'

'I haven't met him but maybe *I* would think him sexy.'

'You would, Kate, you would, but if you found him sinister too would you want to warn her?'

'Well yes, but she wouldn't take any notice of my suspicions would she?'

'She might ... you being a private dick.'

'I couldn't tell her it was just a gut feeling though. I'd have to have some sort of evidence. What is it you think he's done anyway?'

Gill leant forward. 'I think he had a hand in killing Fran and the kids.'

Six

I stared at Gill. She seemed perfectly serious. 'The police,' I said, 'would have investigated things rigorously, especially with two children involved.'

'The police make mistakes.'

'Of course they do. But she walked there...' I broke off, aware I didn't know enough to put forward a really strong case.

'I don't know how he did it but I'm convinced he knows more than he told the police.'

'Give me one good reason, other than the fact you think he's "sinister".'

She was about to answer when we heard Helen's footsteps. 'Tell you later,' she whispered.

'Look what I've got,' said Helen cheerfully, holding up a bottle of champagne. I felt totally sober but I could see the wine had already affected Helen.

We drank the champagne and Gill, undeterred, started asking questions about Paul's plans. I guessed she was probing rather than actually being interested but

Helen remained quite relaxed. 'We will sell this place, I'm sure,' said Helen.

'Does Paul want to stay in Cornwall?' Gill asked casually.

Helen sipped at her champagne. 'He has suggested we honeymoon in Argentina and if I like it we might buy a property out there.'

'Why Argentina?'

'He's got friends out there and he likes the lifestyle and prospects for his work are good.'

'What about your work?'

'Have camera, will travel,' said Helen smiling. Gill slammed her empty glass noisily on the table beside her. She was getting upset, I could see that, so I said, 'Have you got a portfolio, Helen? I'd love to see some of your photos.'

'They're in the study. I'll get them.'

When she'd gone Gill snapped, 'You did that on purpose.'

'Yes. Don't worry, they haven't got definite plans for Argentina.'

'He'll want to do a runner...' She broke off. 'I'll pay you, Kate.'

'Pay me for what?'

'For investigating Paul – like you're a PI – that's what you do for a living isn't it?'

'Yes but – I couldn't ... charge you. I am quite expensive.'

'Money isn't a problem. Just say you'll do it. I'll give you as much help as I can.'

'What do you do for a living, Gill?'

'I've got my own beauty salon.'

'I'm impressed.'

'I had help along the way.'

Neither of us heard Helen come into the room. 'What help was that, Gill?' she asked, moving a low table in front of us and placing two large portfolios there for us to peruse.

Gill gave a little shrug. 'A friend of mine put up the finance.'

'Was that Bernard?'

'No, it was Alan, my previous candy man.'

'Honestly Gill, I don't know why you can't find a nice ordinary man and settle down.'

'You mean like Paul?'

Here we go again, I thought. I feigned real enthusiasm for those photos just to stop them sniping at each other and I was relieved when Gill announced she was shattered and was off to bed. Helen and I followed her a few minutes later. On the way upstairs Helen said, 'Don't think too badly of Gill. She does genuinely care about me and I seem to have so few real friends.'

'I understand. I know she means well.'

That night I fell asleep easily enough only to be wakened not long after. I peered, bleary-eyed at my bedside clock. It was one a.m. and someone was sobbing. Alert and wide awake now I sat on the edge of the bed and listened. Helen was in the room furthest away but Gill was next door. I reasoned it must be Gill. I went to the door, opened it and stood in the hallway. Nothing. An owl hooted and trees rustled but apart from that all was quiet. I returned to bed and tried to dismiss it. Maybe Gill had been crying in her sleep. Perhaps she had problems of her own but if she wanted to share them she would. So, I reasoned, it was none of my business. Strangely I went back to sleep, immediately to be wakened by the unpleasant sound of magpies having some kind of dispute outside my window.

Conversation over breakfast was muted. Helen was pale with slight bags under her eyes but Gill looked fine, no red eyes or puffy cheeks. Maybe the sound had travelled down the hall like some aural illusion. Tamberlake was not haunted by ghosts, I told myself – memories maybe.

It was Gill who drove us to Bude. I was squashed in the back seat but the sun shone and Helen and Gill seemed cheerful enough, except that Gill turned to wink at me a couple of times, which seemed to suggest we were conspirators.

Helen was giving directions and we stopped on the outskirts of Bude, where she pointed to a neat white semi detached in a tree-lined avenue. 'This is it,' she said. We piled out. I'd expected a bog-standard wedding shop so this was a surprise. 'I found her in the local paper,' explained Helen. 'She makes wedding dresses to order. She's brilliant, or so I've heard from someone in the village.'

On the front door was a discreet plaque announcing – *'Your Special Day': Hand-made dresses of distinction. Mrs Lana Blake.*

Mrs Blake answered the door and showed us through to her workroom. She was a small neat woman, about fifty, wearing a plain black dress. Her grey hair was worn in a bun on top of her head and her make-up was subtle. I thought she looked rather chic like a middle-class Parisian. Her accent though was pure East London with no struggle towards being 'proper'. I could see her clients were expected to stay a while, for a tray of tea and biscuits were awaiting us in the bay-windowed conservatory.

'Right, girls. 'Appy days. Who's the lucky bride?'

Helen raised her hand.

'I should 'ave guessed,' she said cheerfully. 'You're the one who looks worried. Never mind, my sweetheart. I'll make you the dress of your dreams. Now, 'ow long 'ave we got?'

'Six weeks.'

'Plenty of time, love. You'll need at least two fittings after this one. Just don't lose any more weight.'

'How did you know I'd lost some?' asked Helen in surprise.

'Brides always do. I reckon they think there's a law about being slim on their wedding day. You can call me Lana – me mother was a fan of Lana Turner.'

We looked a bit blank, never having heard of Lana Turner, so she waved her hand towards the tea tray.

'You two pour the tea and the bride 'ere can 'ave a look at some of my designs.'

Gill and I sat drinking tea and nibbling on biscuits while Helen stripped to her under-wear to try on the samples that Lana pro-duced from a walk-in wardrobe. 'I only 'ave two sizes of each. Brides 'ave an option of returning the dress to me for a three 'undred quid refund after the wedding. Really this is just to see what style you like.'

The first one Helen tried on had huge puffed sleeves and a full skirt. Gill made a puking motion and Lana took one look at Helen in the frothy frock and said firmly, 'Not your style at all, sweetheart.' Hastily Lana helped her out of it and produced a slinky number with neat drapes at its low neckline. A little big across the bust, it still looked sensational. Lana, using pins from a pincushion on her wrist, pinned the top and the waist to fit more snugly. Helen did a twirl, her face shining with happiness. 'Now, that fits you fine and dandy,' said Lana, obviously pleased with her alterations. 'What material do you want? Would you like a motif, a few pearls on the front, and what about the headdress?'

Helen was unsure on all counts. 'Couldn't you just alter this one? I really like it as it is.'

'Wouldn't the groom like you to have a brand-new dress? What's his name? He is a Cornishman, love?'

'Oh yes. He was born at Tamberlake near Trevelly. Paul ... Paul Warrinder.'

Gill and I couldn't fail to notice Lana's reaction. She visibly paled. Helen was oblivious, caught in her own reflection in the full-length mirror.

'Excuse me,' said Lana. 'I'll only be a few minutes.'

Gill glanced at me and flicked her head towards the door. I made my getaway as Gill was suggesting Helen took the dress off and had a cup of tea.

I found Lana in the kitchen smoking a black Turkish cigarette. 'What's the matter?' I asked, getting straight to the point. 'Do you know Paul?'

'No, love. Never met him.' She blew out a stream of smoke and I noticed her colour had now returned to normal.

'What is it then? You may as well tell me. I won't tell the bride.'

'That dress. She can't wear that. It 'as to look different. That was his dead wife's wedding dress. Lovely girl she was. Quite like 'elen. She had bigger boobs but she was the same type – quiet and placid. I couldn't believe it when I read it in the paper. Her and her kiddies too. Bloody tragic. It was all the talk round 'ere – small place, you see.'

'When did she bring the dress back?'

'That was about a year later. She was pregnant then. Not that she showed. I was glad to 'ave it back – nice small size.'

'How did she seem?'

'You mean was she 'appy? Yeah she seemed 'appy enough. She stayed for a cup of tea and said that her 'ubby was often away on business but that she kept busy in the 'ouse and she was looking forward to the birth.'

'And that was the last time you saw her?'

'Yeah. I just read in the papers that she walked over the cliff with the kids in a buggy...' She broke off. 'Whatever made her do that?' she murmured. She stubbed out her cigarette in an ashtray the shape of a shoe. 'You're her friend. What am I going to tell her?'

'Don't worry. We'll persuade her into changing the style a bit. Perhaps if we say she'll look better in cream. And we'll concentrate on the headdress. Leave it with us. A day or so.'

'Right you are, love. It did give me a bit of a turn – just imagine if 'e turns up at the wedding and there she is wearing 'is dead wife's dress.'

Helen, in the conservatory, still in blissful ignorance, had produced a notepad and was designing her own headdress. Gill looked uncomfortable and was obviously dying to know what was going on.

I admired Helen's designs and after about twenty minutes we were ready to leave. Helen and Gill walked ahead and I lagged behind. 'Give me a ring tomorrow, love,' Lana whispered. 'There's something I need to tell you. Only gossip really but you never know.'

Seven

That evening Helen gave Gill and me no chance to talk alone. Gill was twitchy the whole evening and we both made our excuses to go to bed relatively early. About midnight I crept next door to Gill's room. She was sitting up in bed wide awake.

'Sit down,' she said impatiently, 'and tell me what all that bother was with Lana.' I told her about the dress and about Lana asking me to phone her.

'Now do you believe me?' she asked.

'The dress is only a ghastly coincidence. It doesn't say anything about Paul does it?'

'If you met him you'd understand.'

'Would I? I think you're more of an expert on men than I am. The men I attract look as if they've just stepped out of a Hovis advert.'

'Safe though,' said Gill with a slight smile.

'What exactly do you suspect Paul of? OK, he was away on business a great deal. He may have been blind to Fran's unhappiness but most men live in blinkers where women are concerned. It means he was an average husband.'

'What about the fact he keeps the attic locked? Helen told me that was a habit he'd got into when the children were alive, as he didn't want them rampaging around.'

'So? That's seems reasonable enough.'

Gill frowned at me. 'Strange he takes the key with him. There *are* no children now.'

'Yes,' I agreed, 'but, if you've noticed, there aren't any photographs of Fran or the children anywhere. Maybe the attic room is a shrine to them and he doesn't want Helen being reminded all the time.'

'Well I think he must have been born from a pea pod,' she said, 'because there are no photos of him either or his parents. That seems strange to me.'

'Come off it, Gill. You're being paranoid now. I'm sure he's got his faults. He may be the jealous and possessive type, he may be focused on his job, but that still doesn't make him the devil incarnate.'

Gill wouldn't be deterred. 'Let's talk about his job. That's all a bit woolly isn't it? Financial advisor – going off to Argentina to play polo and yet this dump has had hardly any money spent on it in years.'

'Perhaps the house isn't a priority any-more. He does want to sell it, after all.'

'Well he hasn't tried very hard is all I can say.'

Gill seemed to be getting more wound up rather than less. Perhaps because her arguments didn't stand up under any sort of rational scrutiny. But then how often had I gone with gut instinct rather than logic and rationality? I tried being conciliatory. 'We obviously can't stop Helen marrying him but we can be there for her if things go wrong. After all, Fran was seemingly happily married to him for five years.'

'She wasn't that happy was she? She committed suicide and took the children with her. Obviously she didn't think Paul would look after them properly.'

'I don't think that stands up. The children were very young; her bond with them would have been far stronger. And, being depressed and probably deluded, she thought they should stay with her.'

'Well,' said Gill dully. 'We don't know anything about Fran or her state of mind do we?'

I had to agree that we didn't. But Gill wasn't going to let things drop and I was tired and getting worn down. 'OK, Gill, you win. I'll take on the case. I have to warn you, though, I'm not brilliant. I'll do my best. After all, I've nothing to lose. I'm not on a job at the moment. I'll try and find out as much as I can.'

Gill threw her arms around me and kissed me on both cheeks. 'I'll pay you well,' she said, insisting on giving me a cheque there and then.

'Just expenses only,' I said as she began writing out the cheque. 'This is one for old times' sake.'

Her idea of 'expenses' was very generous. If the investigation lasted for months I'd have to cash it but otherwise I wouldn't be taking it to the bank just yet.

Back in my room I immediately regretted agreeing. I was even beginning to feel a little sorry for Paul. After all, he had lost his wife and children in tragic circumstances. He'd found a new love and enjoyed playing polo. Did he really deserve someone trying to rake over his past? It'll be all right, I thought, as long as he doesn't find out that I've been snooping. So far he hardly knew I existed and as long as neither Helen nor Gill told him I was a private investigator he need never know.

Hubert had sent me a text message. '*When back?*' Good question I thought. Tomorrow was Wednesday. I decided to give it one more day.

The next morning Helen was on good form. The sun was shining and she planned a picnic and she wanted to take a few shots for the Tourist Board. While she and Gill beavered away in the kitchen packing the picnic basket I returned to my room to phone Lana.

'It's only a bit of gossip, love,' she began, 'but being in the wedding trade I do keep in touch with the competition. It's a few years back now but a friend of mine kitted this girl out with an expensive ready-made dress. Anyway the day she was due to collect it she rang to say the wedding was off and she wouldn't be requiring the dress. So my friend felt sorry for 'er and offered 'er all the money back and she sent 'er a cheque.'

I was about to ask what that had to do with Helen and Paul when she added, 'It was Paul Warrinder, see, and she was living at Tamberlake.'

'How long was this before he married Fran?'

'Barely six months – fast worker eh?'

'And what happened to the prospective bride?'

'That's just the point. Ali was her name, short for Alison – Alison Peters. She was never seen again.'

'Well I suppose if her relationship was over she wouldn't hang around, would she?'

'No, probably not, but it seems bloody odd to me she didn't cash that cheque.'

It seemed bloody odd to me too and I quickly decided not to tell Gill the whole story. She'd be foaming at the mouth if I did. So I decided to say that Paul had a live-in girlfriend before meeting Fran. It was years ago anyway and surely she couldn't get uptight about *that*.

We were sitting on Ilfracombe beach when

I told her. Helen had got off with her camera and we sat well fed and sleepy, letting the sand slip through our toes and watching children paddling. Gill seemed relaxed and wasn't surprised about there being another woman. 'She could be a good source of information couldn't she?'

'Well yes,' I acknowledged. 'I suppose she could.'

'Where is she now?'

'I've no idea.'

Gill fell silent for a while and then said, 'If we could get into that attic room I'm sure we could find out a bit more about his past.'

'How can we do that without a key?'

She looked at me pityingly as if I had no right to call myself a private detective.

'We hire a criminal, perhaps a bent locksmith.'

'Do you know someone?'

'Helen says she knows a man who does.'

A sudden breeze from the sea made me shiver. Above me the once blue skies had started changing to a motley of grey. It was the end of the conversation. We hurriedly brushed sand from our feet and packed away the picnic debris. A downpour seemed imminent and we looked for shelter; so, as it seemed, did everyone else on the beach. It was then that I spotted Helen, camera slung over her shoulder, walking briskly towards us and within minutes we were in the car just as the deluge started.

The storm that followed was intense. Gill had to come off the road because conditions were so atrocious. 'Where's the ark?' said Gill cheerfully as we watched the torrential rain and forked lightning. I believe that because cars have rubber wheels a car is one of the safest places to be in a storm but I wasn't totally convinced. Surely it couldn't be safer than under the duvet?

When the rain eased so that Gill could actually see the road she drove off at a stately pace and eventually we approached Tamberlake. Although a totally different style to Norman Bates's house in Hitchcock's *Psycho*, in pouring rain, thunder and lightning it looked grim and foreboding. But then it was a big, old house not a Barratt's starter home, although, if I was getting married, I know which I would have preferred.

Over supper I told Helen I would be leaving the next day. I lied through my teeth about my landlord wanting me to return because veritable queues of clients were awaiting my services. I expected her to object but she merely said, 'Oh that's a shame. But you'll be coming back won't you?' When I explained I lived above my landlord's premises I failed to be prepared for the inevitable question. The words 'funeral director' caused wine-fuelled giggles, and I found myself hotly defending Hubert and his noble profession.

'You two really don't know what's involved – do you?' I said shirtily. I then told them an undertaker was a cross between a diplomat and a father confessor and that Hubert organized everything, flowers, presentation of the body, catering and even giving advice on finance and benefits. They still giggled and asked if Hubert was attractive. I said not to me but that my mother had enjoyed a mild fling with him.

They were still giggling when I decided to go to bed. Storms have an effect on some people or so I've heard, rather like a full moon, so I tried to excuse both of them on those grounds but I was still irritated.

I rang Hubert from my bedroom to say I'd be back early evening. He said Jasper had missed me and was I on a case?

'Yes,' I said.

'Good. I need a laugh,' he answered.

I almost wished I hadn't defended him quite so vigorously but I did look forward to going home.

The next morning I was in the middle of a dream when I woke with a start to find Gill standing by my bed. 'Caught you!' she said smiling. I wasn't amused. I was still bemused by my dream.

'What's going on?'

'Nothing,' said Gill cheerfully. 'I just thought I'd wake you up. It's gone nine o'clock and I wanted to speak to you alone.' I struggled to sit up and gather my wits but they seemed more scattered than usual this morning. 'I've found our man,' she said with a note of triumph.

Still witless I said, 'What are you talking about?'

She tutted like an irritable schoolteacher. 'The man to open the attic door. Included in the price he says he'll do us two spare keys.'

'Oh good,' I said as I slid my legs out of bed to sit on the edge. All I really wanted was a cup of hot tea. Gill meanwhile was on full throttle.

'I'll take Helen out in the car somewhere and leave the back door open for him. He says it'll only take him an hour or so to bring back the duplicate keys, which he'll leave for us under a stone by the bird pond.'

'Very cloak and dagger,' I said. 'So he's local?'

'Yeah. I spun him a yarn and paid him well so he's happy.'

I wasn't happy, because it had occurred to me that he couldn't make a duplicate key without some sort of impression. I'd seen films where they made an impression from soap. So how was he going to do it? The man was obviously a criminal and what if he robbed the place or was 'casing the joint' for someone else? But it was too late now.

'What time is he coming?' I asked.

'Eleven-ish,' said Gill. 'Why?'

'I'll pretend to leave just before you take Helen out. Then I'll double back and keep an eye on him.'

'I'm sure we can trust him,' said Gill looking peeved. 'I've told him to leave the door open for you.'

'Never trust a criminal,' I said, sounding just like Hubert giving me one of his warnings. 'I'll be there to make sure he doesn't plan to make a complete set of house keys.'

By ten forty-five Gill was sitting in her car ready to drive Helen off on a bridal-shoe hunt followed by another hunt for a 'going away' outfit. I'd already put my holdall in the car when Helen gave me a hug. 'I'll be in touch. You must meet Paul before the wedding and I'm planning a hen night. Now promise me you'll come.'

'I'll certainly try.'

'I'll make sure she does,' said Gill glancing at her watch and starting up the engine. She drove off as I sat in my car.

I decided I should leave the car tucked away at the far side of the house where chummy wouldn't see it. Then I lurked in the bushes hoping it wouldn't be too long before he arrived.

He was on time. My first view was a short man of about sixty with a slight paunch, balding but with strong tanned legs. His shorts were khaki, a sort of half-combat style. As far as appearance went he was a fourth-division criminal.

But he was first division on speed. Within ten minutes he'd reappeared from the house and driven off. I waited for a few moments and then made my way to the house.

At the attic door I paused. I turned the old-fashioned round handle. It was open and I was in.

Eight

Two skylights flooded the large room with light. The sloping ceilings gave the room character, otherwise it was fairly bleak. I stood for a moment looking round trying to find the measure of the man who kept this room locked. On the left-hand side against the wall was a desk. On the desk was a single photograph, which from the doorway looked like Helen. In the corner on the right-hand side were two vast cardboard boxes of the type used for moving house. And facing me was a sofa bed above which were heavily laden bookshelves.

I went straight to the bookshelves. The bulk of the books were either about wine-making or polo or South America. I searched in vain for any books that might have belonged to Fran or the children. There were none.

Next I opened the desk drawers; there were three on each side. One contained thin files, each one neatly labelled – gas, electricity, water, car, mortgage. The mortgage file I read quickly. He'd taken out a new loan in the first year of his marriage for £100,000 on a six per cent fixed loan over five years. It was in his name only. The next file I came across was one labelled *Bank*. There were only his two latest bank statements in it. His current account contained £5,000 and regular varying amounts kept it topped up. I wished I had a camera, that way I could have examined everything at my leisure. Figures are not a strong point of mine but even so the irregular sums and varying times of the month and sources *did* indicate someone working freelance. His outgoings seemed to be utilities and the mortgage. There was a credit-card bill on which he owed £8,000 and which was paid regularly. Mostly the amounts were for expensive restaurant meals, some of the names of which I recognized from TV. He'd also paid a yearly subscription to a London gym.

In one drawer there were pens and notepads, stamps and elastic bands. I used a sheet of paper and a pen to write down the name of the gym and one or two of the restaurants.

In the remaining drawers was a folder with his birth and his marriage certificate and various other certificates such as his GCE 'O' levels and his four 'A' levels, all at grade A. Bright lad, I thought, and tidy too. Far too tidy. I looked in vain for photographs of Fran and the children. But in the last drawer I struck lucky. Under a pile of maps – there it was – a passport. His passport. Five years old. He'd been to Argentina several times and Bolivia. I was a bit uptight now. Who the hell was this man and what the hell was he up to?

After that I concentrated on the two cardboard boxes. The first box contained watercolours about a foot square wrapped carefully in bubble wrap. I took two or three out. I'm not much of an art buff but to me they looked very good. There in the right-hand corner was the signature P. Warrinder. He'd obviously given up painting now for there was no evidence of easels or brushes or paints. In the other box were unwrapped paintings, equally good but with one major difference – the signature. This time they were signed F. Warrinder. They were unmistakably by the same artist. He wasn't the artist – Fran had been the artist and, to my eyes, she'd been talented. And he was altering her signature.

It was then I made a decision. I was going to 'borrow' one painting from each box. I planned to get an expert opinion on them. I was making my choice from the bubble-wrapped ones when a sliver of folded paper fell out. Someone had been playing with it and rolling it into a long cigarette shape. I rolled it out flat. It was the instructions and warnings of an antidepressant called *Tourine*.

I'd never heard of it. I folded the paper properly and slipped it into the pocket of my jeans. I glanced at my watch. I'd been in the attic nearly an hour – if our 'crim' was as prompt as previously, he'd be back with the duplicate key any minute.

There was one more thing I had to do before leaving the house. I wanted to check out the master bedroom. I was rushing now to have a quick reconnoitre into Paul's wardrobe. It was an oak double-door monstrosity with a deep drawer underneath. Inside, I was surprised to find at least a score of expensive suits and shirts. He wasn't into ready-mades from M&S. I had a quick peep into Helen's wardrobe and was surprised to find some expensive labels there too.

I wanted to spend more time in the bedroom but the sound of a vehicle driving up the gravel path stopped me in my tracks. I watched surreptitiously from the window and saw the little man come into the house. I stood stock still as he came up the stairs. I heard him climb to the attic, and then seconds later he was closing the back door. I saw him lift a large stone near the birdbath and then he paused to look up at the house before he walked briskly to his white van and drove off. His name was emblazoned on the side – *Robert Roberts – Handyman and General Repairs*.

I left the house then, leaving just one more

job to do before leaving Cornwall, collect the local newspapers of two years ago.

I left the office with a bundle of newspapers, which had been left ready for me. I paid for them and the elderly porter at the door waved to me saying in a broad impenetrable accent, 'Don't you read all them at once my beauty, you'll go blind.'

The journey back to Longborough took two hours more than going, mainly due to roadworks, and I was exhausted when I eventually arrived back at five p.m. In the car park a Daimler was being polished by one of the pallbearers, who doubles as the car man. I only knew him as Bill. He was shouting something to me. I got out of the car. 'He's not well. The boss. Not well at all. I reckon he needs a doctor.'

'Right, thanks, Bill,' I said. 'I'll see to it.'

I hurried upstairs without my luggage. Hubert was never ill. I rushed to his flat and found him in bed with the curtains pulled. I could hardly see him the room was so dark. At first I thought he was unconscious. But the light seemed to rouse him and Jasper, who was on the far side of the bed. Jasper's whole body shook and quivered in greeting. Hubert meanwhile lay puce-coloured and sweating badly. He saw me and had trouble focusing his eyes but he managed to raise his hand, only to start coughing uncontrollably.

He tried to raise himself but sank back against the pillows. 'I'm going to ring the doctor now,' I said. He didn't seem to hear me but when the coughing fit was over he closed his eyes and appeared to fall asleep.

A lanky young locum turned up at six p.m. – listened to Hubert's chest – announced it was 'something going around' but prescribed antibiotics just in case it was pneumonia. Plenty of clear fluids and analgesics every four hours, that was the usual mantra but as he left he said, 'If his breathing worsens get your husband to hospital.'

'He's not my husband.'

'OK – partner.'

I shot him an angry look.

'Well, whoever he is it's the same advice,' he said as he rushed through the door. I swore under my breath as he left.

Later when I'd had the prescription filled I plied Hubert with an assortment of medication and insisted he drank squash by the pint. I sponged his face and hands and then left him alone to sleep. Over the next couple of hours he coughed every few minutes but I could see his temperature had reduced and he was well enough for me to leave him while I walked Jasper.

During the walk my mobile rang twice. Perhaps not being able to carry on a conversation in the street with any ease is a sign of growing older but I found it difficult. The first call was from my mother. I think she was trying to tell me she was getting itchy feet. Megan it seems was being visited quite a bit by David and I think she was tiring of playing gooseberry. I told her I'd ring her the next day and that I wouldn't be driving over, because Hubert was poorly. Telling her was a mistake. 'I'll get a taxi tomorrow morning,' she said, 'and come over and cheer him up.'

A few minutes later Gill rang. 'What did you find?' she asked excitedly.

'I can't talk now,' I said, 'I'm walking the dog. When you get a chance to see the room tonight ring me and tell me what you make of it all.'

'Anytime?'

I knew I wouldn't be getting much sleep so I agreed, 'Yes, anytime.'

On my return from Jasper's walk I collected my holdall and the Cornish newspapers from the car and went upstairs to find Hubert struggling to get out of bed. 'I don't know what you gave me,' he said. 'But I'm feeling much better. I fancy a sandwich.'

'I'll fetch you a sandwich,' I said. 'But you must stay in bed.'

He lay back. 'I'm so glad you're back. I could have died.'

'Don't exaggerate. Anyway I'll be needing some help on this case.'

'Is this the big one?'

Hubert always thought one of my cases –

'the big one' – would rescue me from minor cases to the 'big time', whatever that was, in private investigation circles. Sometimes I think he becomes confused between fact and fiction. After all, who could name a real-life private investigator?

A ham sandwich seemed to settle Hubert and I left him with his medication and instructions to shout loudly if he needed me. 'What if I can't summon the strength?' he asked.

'Tough!'

'You're a hard woman.'

'No. I just don't want you milking this illness for all it's worth.'

'Have I been ill before?'

'No.'

'Well then have some sympathy.'

'Just keep drinking the squash and you'll pull through.'

As I walked back to my flat I realized we were getting more like a bickering married couple every day. It was time, I told myself, I found a man. But I hadn't had much luck so far. A little voice in the back of my head said, *Put some effort in and you might.* Another little voice answered, *You're far too busy at the moment.*

Gill rang at one a.m. I was half-asleep but roused myself. Strangely she seemed disappointed. 'There wasn't much, was there?' she said.

'Less is more in this case,' I said. 'No photos or diaries. Nothing to suggest Fran and the children ever existed. Which in itself is odd. And what about the paintings?'

'They're good. He's quite talented.'

'You didn't notice then that he altered the signatures?'

There was a momentary silence. 'You must think I'm stupid, Kate. I only looked at the top few in the box.'

'And,' I said. 'You haven't mentioned the passport.'

'What passport?'

'The one in the third drawer under the maps.'

There was a short silence. 'I looked,' said Gill. 'I couldn't find a passport.'

'You'll have to go back and have another look.'

'Is it Helen's?'

'No it's Paul's.'

I heard Gill's little gasp of surprise. 'So he hasn't gone to Argentina?'

'I suppose he could have,' I said. 'On a false passport. Or he's somewhere in the UK.'

'The bastard has got another woman.'

'Don't let's jump to any conclusions. If you can't find that passport it must mean Helen's taken it.'

'It's got to be there. It's got to be.' Gill was beginning to sound frantic now. 'Helen's so straight,' she added, 'she'd hand in a dropped pound coin.'

I wasn't sure I believed that but I murmured in agreement just to appease her.

'The only other possibility,' I suggested, 'and it's very remote, is that Robert Roberts nipped back after I'd left and stole it. But that's verging on the ridiculous – what motive could he possibly have?'

'Well...'

'Well what?'

'You see he's not a criminal,' she said. 'He's an ex-cop. I actually told him the truth.'

I sighed, not really being sure about the implications. 'OK – let's not panic. You go and recheck the attic and don't forget to lock the door. Ring me back from there and let me know.'

'You mean now?' asked Gill, sounding surprised.

'Yes. What's Paul going to do if he returns and finds his passport missing?'

'Who bloody cares?'

'I expect Helen will. We both think he's a dodgy character, so we don't want to put her in any danger do we?'

Silence. 'I hadn't looked at it that way,' she said thoughtfully. 'I'll go up there now.'

'Ring me in half an hour, I need to check on Hubert.'

'Will do. Thanks, Kate.'

I crept along to Hubert's room, my mind

in turmoil. Thankfully he was asleep.

One hour later with the newspaper reports of the tragedy laid out on my bed Gill still hadn't phoned. Had Helen caught her in the act? Should I ring her? I tried to concentrate on reading but couldn't. After a further fifteen minutes I dialled Gill's mobile. There was no answer.

Nine

I folded up the newspapers, tried one more time to contact Gill and then gave up on the day. I was exhausted and worried but there was nothing I could do.

In the morning I took Hubert a mug of tea and he looked more chipper. 'Hardly coughed last night,' he said proudly. He peered at me. 'Did you have a good night?'

I shook my head. 'I'll tell you all about it later.'

I took Jasper for a walk and felt far more wide awake when I got back. I was just boiling an egg for Hubert's breakfast when my mobile rang. It was Gill sounding agitated. 'Kate, I'm really, really sorry. I was creeping past Helen's room and I heard her sobbing. I couldn't just ignore it could I?'

'What was wrong with her?'

'Something about a man she'd met in India. A journalist. A brief affair and it turns out he was married.'

'So are you saying she's got pre-wedding nerves?'

'Well sort of – this ex-love has got in touch

100

to say his wife is divorcing him and he wants to carry on where they left off.'

'I wonder why she didn't mention him before in our girly chats.'

'Well, you know Helen, she likes everyone to think she's a bit of a lady. A married journo doesn't fit her image.'

'I think that's the point I want to make, Gill. I *don't* know her. She once wore the whitest of white socks, her mother died of cancer, she's a great cook and she enjoys travelling. For a living she takes photos and in her wardrobe she has some very expensive clothes. That is really all I know – well – except she's in love with Paul Warrinder or says she is.'

'You sound suspicious of her,' she said after a long pause.

'I wouldn't put it as strongly as that. Just curious about her motivation.'

'What do you mean?'

'Well, is it real love or is she searching for security?'

'Better security with a fantastic-looking rich guy than an old fat ugly one. And believe me I know what I'm talking about.'

'Does she see any faults in him at all?'

'Not really. Although she did say tonight she thought he was secretive.'

'It seems Helen may have some secrets too.'

'I'm very fond of Helen,' said Gill sharply.

'I know. But how well do you know her? How often have you seen her since school?'

Gill's sharp tone changed now. 'I suppose twice a year. We've kept in touch by e-mail and phone.'

'I don't want to upset you, Gill, but she may not be the person you think she is.'

'You're just cynical.'

'No, it's being in the investigation business. It's like a woman in labour. It's not a normal birth till it's over. I'm struggling not to make two and two equal a villain without having proof.'

'You'll find the proof. He is the villain. Don't try to make Helen out as some sort of accomplice.'

'I wasn't.'

Strange that now she'd used the word accomplice it actually put the idea in my head.

'What about the passport, Gill?' I asked.

'Oh ... I found it. Didn't I say? It was tucked in one of those magazines.'

She didn't lie well. But I couldn't carry on the conversation knowing that she thought it necessary to lie to protect her friend.

'When you want to tell me the truth, Gill – ring me again. Bye.'

I could almost sense her shock that I hadn't been taken in by her feeble lie. The passport was missing. Helen was the chief suspect. If she was protecting Paul the question was – why? What had he done? Or, more to the point, what was he up to now?

Two days later Gill still hadn't rung. My mother, though, had visited Hubert bearing grapes and lemon barley water. I noticed she was reverting back to type, her skirts were getting shorter and her make-up heavier. She would undoubtedly be on the move again soon. Hubert, though, seemed to rally in her presence and she spent a few hours with him playing cards. Maybe, if my mother was off on her travels, I'd see more of Megan and Katy, but from my mother's observations David Todman had more than a foot in the door now and I didn't fancy playing gooseberry either.

As far as investigating Paul Warrinder was concerned I had found out something. I'd phoned Helen to thank her for her hospitality. I'd caught her in the garden. 'I'm a bit worried about Gill,' she said. 'She seems really preoccupied and she's obsessed with finding fault with Paul. Do you think she's jealous?'

'She might be,' I said. 'He's young and gorgeous. Who wouldn't be? When's he coming back from Argentina?'

'There's a problem. It could be next week now. But Gill, bless her, has promised she'll stay until he gets back.'

'So, you don't feel any better about staying

in the house alone?'

'I wish I did, Kate. I haven't heard anything ... creepy ... since I've had company but there's something making me very uneasy.'

'Is Paul likely to go abroad often?'

'Yes he is.'

'Why don't you stay in a hotel when he's away?'

'I'd be happy doing that but he says the house needs someone in it and he likes to picture me at Tamberlake.'

I swallowed hard. I wanted to say, *Come on Helen. Stop being such a wimp.* Helen wasn't stupid. She simply wanted to please and I couldn't help feeling he was taking advantage of her. Perhaps I was slow but it suddenly occurred to me that I'd taken it for granted that all three of us were scraping a living. Gill, as it turned out, had her 'candy man' and, thanks to him, her own business. And I didn't suppose photos of Cornwall and Wales brought in that much. The house had been remortgaged and Paul wasn't in Argentina, so the rich playboy scenario wasn't a sure thing. Helen had a wardrobe of designer labels. The question remained. Did Helen have money?

Asking outright about her bank account seemed intrusive, so we finished the conversation on a chat about wedding shoes and the headdress. Helen promised to ring me soon and badger me about coming down for the weekend to meet Paul. I murmured that I'd look forward to that.

Now that the wedding outfit was complete, it was all systems go. I felt like a Judas because it looked likely that Helen was going to find out some unpalatable information about her beloved. The main question being would it be best for her to know before the wedding or after? Logically it would be better for her to have any information before the wedding but emotionally she could be heartbroken.

I did need to speak to Gill again. She had knowledge of Helen's friends and family that I didn't have. I'd just have to apologize and say that being suspicious wasn't a choice for me; it was a lifestyle.

Hubert, thank goodness, was by now up and about. He was already fretting about his backlog of funerals but he wasn't quite fit enough to put in a full day. He was, however, in need of some mental stimulation, or so he said, and I needed some input from him.

We sat in the kitchen drinking coffee and I told him that I was on a genuine investigation. He smiled. 'In contrast to your fake investigations.'

I bristled at that. 'I need you to be serious,' I said. 'Helen could be in some sort of danger.'

'Right,' he said. 'Tell me the story from the

beginning and my poor addled brain might just about cope.'

I told him about the house first.

'Do you think it's haunted?' he asked.

'No, definitely not.'

'Well, we know Helen's scared on her own there,' he said thoughtfully. 'I suppose that's because she knows another woman was unhappy enough to kill herself and take her children with her...' He paused and I was about to chip in when he said, 'What about him – the widower?'

'What do you mean?'

'Is he scared of the place? Does he think it's haunted?'

There were times, I thought, when a male perspective opened up a whole range of different concepts. I didn't of course know the answer to Hubert's question. And he looked somewhat smug. 'That business with the passport and not being in Argentina might just be his way of escaping from the house and its memories. He might not want to admit he's scared shitless too.'

'I suppose that's a possibility,' I grudgingly admitted. I did know he'd tried to sell the house but was that for his sake or Helen's? 'But he's obviously dishonest or why would he want to pass off Fran's paintings as his own? He could have sold those anyway.'

'I don't know the answer to that,' said Hubert. 'Let me read the newspaper reports and see if I can make any sense of it. Perhaps the reporter on the local rag could give you some more information.'

I flashed Hubert a huge smile.

'What did I say?' he asked, mystified.

'You just gave me an idea. Thanks.'

I rushed off then to get him the Cornish newspapers. On my return he sat with a pen and a notepad poised. He seemed pleased enough to have something to do and the thought struck me that I'd read the reports when I was half-asleep. Had I missed anything? I'd be mortified if Hubert proved he was more observant than me and judging by the determined look on his face he was out to do just that.

I took Jasper for a walk and rang Gill's mobile from a bench by the river. 'I can't talk now, sweetie,' she said. 'I'll ring you later.' Obviously Helen was around and she couldn't talk normally. Gill reserved her generic 'sweeties' for all males, just in case she slipped up.

Viewing Hubert from the kitchen doorway on my return I noticed he was making copious notes. Jasper, undecided about whom to stay with, followed me to my office, where I labelled a file and decided to call it 'Tamberlake'. I then began a list of people I needed to talk to. I put Paul Warrinder at the top of the list but I needed far more background before I met him. That way I might be able to tell truth from lies.

Gill's suspicions that somehow Paul had a hand in his family's death didn't gel with me but I conceded that he might well have caused her mental breakdown by something he did or something she found out. All the conjecture in the world wasn't going to make any difference and the moment Hubert was fully better I was going to find Paul Warrinder.

'Stop lurking in the doorway and come in.' Hubert it seems could see through the back of his head. I was impressed until I realized he could see my reflection in the murky kitchen window. The window cleaner had also been laid low with the 'bug' with no name and consequently they hadn't been cleaned for three weeks.

'Did you read these reports properly?' Hubert asked.

'I was tired,' I said, 'and there didn't seem much information.'

'That's a point I wanted to make. Take this line – "*Friends of the couple were too upset to talk about the deaths but the local delicatessen owner said they were a very sociable couple who often entertained.*" '

'OK, so their friends didn't want to talk to the press.'

'Ask yourself why not?'

'I don't know.'

'And the funeral?'

'What about it?'

'It says here–' he jabbed at the paper '–"*The small church of St Peter's was packed to capacity.*" '

'So?'

'So, you need to get back to Cornwall and talk to their friends.'

'I did realize that,' I snapped.

'Well, I think you'll need help,' said Hubert, staring at me over his reading glasses. 'I could get in touch with the under-taker and get some inside info.'

'That would be great,' I said, with no real enthusiasm. Hubert it seemed was trying to hijack my case.

'I was thinking,' said Hubert, 'it would probably be best if I actually came with you.' I stared at him. Hubert didn't 'do' absence from his business, unless it was the annual Funeral Directors' Convention. 'I'll have to get a locum in,' he added, 'but I'm prepared to take a week or so off, because I think this is an important case.'

'Do you? I think you think I'll cock it up.'

'No I don't. And I need some fresh sea air. I'm not feeling a hundred per cent.'

'That's it, Hubert – tug at my heart strings.'

I did of course need some help. I patted Hubert on the cheek and said we'd be off first thing in the morning. 'I'll do the driv-ing,' I said and Hubert muttered something about sharing it but at least it was settled.

Gill rang at eleven thirty. She sounded subdued and I thought that was because she harboured some resentment for my calling her a liar. 'I'm sorry I didn't believe you,' I said. 'If you say the passport wasn't there and then mysteriously it was there, then I accept that you were telling the truth.'

'I'm sorry, Kate. I did lie about finding it again. Only Helen could have removed it. I regret that now ... I've found out something else. I haven't let Helen know but quite honestly she's not the person I thought she was and I don't know if I can stay here any longer.' Her tone was so different now from the cheerful bouncy Gill who'd arrived at Tamberlake only a few days before. She sounded near to tears. 'Come on,' I said softly. 'Tell me what you've found out.'

Ten

Gill sniffed and took a sighing breath. 'I was looking through Helen's personal photos. Just out of interest. Everything was there, all in order, neat writing underneath. Family photos, school days, first job, old boyfriends, days out, days by the sea in ... Cornwall. And there amongst all those important moments was a photo of her sitting on a wall behind Fran and her children on the beach. I guess it was Paul taking the photo. She was smiling as if he were taking a photo of her.'

'Don't jump to conclusions, Gill. It may have been a coincidence. Were there any other photos of them together?'

'Not that I found,' she said, then added in a rush, 'I won't sleep tonight. I didn't sleep last night. I think this house is evil. There's something I can't explain. I haven't heard anything but I can feel it. There's a presence and I think that there is something we need to do but I don't know what it is.' I was quite worried. She was getting distraught and I wasn't sure what to say to make her feel better.

'Calm down,' I said. 'Take a deep breath. You have got an option. Leave there and take Helen with you. Book into a B&B.'

'She won't leave. She says she's got to get used to it...' She broke off. 'I just don't trust her anymore.'

'I'm coming down tomorrow with Hubert, my landlord. We'll probably stay somewhere near Tamberlake. You and I can meet up if you can shake Helen off.'

'Yeah, OK.' She sounded reluctant. Then she added, 'I wish I'd never got involved in all this. My fault ... I want to cling on to the past.'

'I'll ring you tomorrow,' I said. 'If you call me "sweetie" I'll know Helen's around.'

I found Hubert in my office using my computer. 'I'm finding us a hotel,' he said. 'Nice-looking place near Trevelly. Food a specialty. That'll suit you.'

'Food doesn't rule my life.'

'Keeps you happy though doesn't it?'

I smiled sweetly, refusing to rise to his bait. 'I'm off to get packed. Are we taking Jasper, by the way?'

'Of course. They allow small dogs in the ground-floor rooms.'

'Good. I'm off to get packed.'

'I thought we'd make an early start,' said Hubert. 'Six a.m.'

'Fine. What car?'

'Mine's the best.'

'Well it would be wouldn't it?'

Even I was impressed when I saw a white Porsche parked outside. 'You haven't bought this have you?' I asked.

'Well I didn't steal it. It arrived while you were away. I haven't had a chance to give it a spin.'

'Are you sure you're well enough to drive?' I was, of course, only angling to drive it myself.

Hubert grinned. 'It'll be less tiring to drive it myself.'

The drive itself was slow and tedious. Hubert didn't plan to wear out his new car by thrashing it at speeds above 60 mph, but I have to admit it was such a comfortable drive that I slept between our regular comfort breaks.

The hotel when we finally arrived at one o'clock was, I thought, 'twee' – all bone china cups and saucers, lace doilies and elderly couples enjoying 'civilization' at the 'Regis'.

The receptionist, a brightly painted woman in her forties, spoke in a loud high voice. 'Lunch is being served now,' she trilled. 'And this evening dinner is served at seven p.m. precisely, there's bingo at eight in the small ballroom, followed by live music.'

'I can hardly wait,' I said. Hubert and the receptionist looked daggers at me. Jasper tried to wriggle free from under Hubert's arms and we made a hasty exit to our ground-floor rooms.

The room itself overlooked the garden and there were sliding doors leading outside. It was a bit chintzy for my taste but the bed looked and felt fine and it was roomy. It was certainly more cheerful than the guest room at Tamberlake. Hubert announced he was pleased with his room and with the enclosed garden, because he could leave the door open and let Jasper run free.

Luckily we were assigned a table for two. There was a moderate choice of menu but it was three courses and the other diners seemed to be enjoying large portions. 'Have you ever noticed,' I asked Hubert, 'how well pensioners eat?'

'It's senior citizens now. You're already in training aren't you?'

I ignored his jibe. 'It does make you wonder about healthy eating, though, because I've noticed old people love biscuits and cakes and red meat and pies. How come it's done them no harm?'

'I dunno, Kate. They were the generation who only had fresh fruit if someone was ill in the house. Seems surprising they got past forty. I'm surprised I'm still here, I was brought up on suet dumplings and bread and dripping with salt.'

After the gut-busting lunch I felt like sleeping but Hubert had his agenda. 'First stop,' he said, 'the deli in Trevelly.' I wondered why that was his first stop but since he was the man with the car I didn't have much choice. I had a nervous twitch in my stomach, or was it a foreboding that Hubert really was taking over my case? Or maybe I'd simply eaten too much. Either way I felt a bit sick.

The delicatessen, tucked away in a side street, reminded me of shops in Spain or France – small but stocked to the gunnels – decorated with hams and salamis and sausage of every nationality. Those that couldn't be hung up were displayed on the marble counters covered with domed glass. Cheeses of the world were arranged with tiny bunches of black and white grapes between them. Virgin olive oils labelled as well as any wine were packed in ranks on the shelves, along with every known variety of vinegar.

There were no other customers and the owner – a big bearded man in his fifties wearing a white apron – seemed delighted we'd appeared. 'I'm Rufus,' he said. His accent, although hard to place, was not West Country. 'Are you on holiday?' he asked Hubert. For some reason he ignored me completely.

'I'm looking for olive oil,' answered Hubert. 'A good one,' he added. I was surprised, I knew that recently Hubert had occasionally used olive oil, influenced by tales of everlasting youth, but I had no idea he was going to use it as a tactic. In Hubert's youth olive oil was for purely medicinal purposes. It was warmed, poured on cotton wool and then inserted into the ear to relieve earache.

They went into a cosy huddle and then Rufus took a bottle of olive oil from the top shelf and gave Hubert a short lecture on second and third 'pressings' and would he like a taster on a piece of bread? Hubert did and I was about to intervene in this leisurely form of shopping when Hubert asked Rufus, 'How long have you had the shop?'

He smiled good-naturedly. 'I'd like to say this was the family business and I'd been here all my life. But I worked in the city, sold the London house and bought this four years ago. A dream come true.'

Hubert nodded sagely. I moved slightly nearer to both of them and Rufus smiled at me as if suddenly realizing that I was there. 'Try this new cheese, my dear – lovely dessert cheese – white Stilton with ginger.'

He cut me off a rather large sample and I nibbled away while Hubert came up with the reason for our visit. 'I paid a visit to Tamberlake, near Trevelly, a few years back.'

'Did you really? Lovely house. Run-down now I suppose. So tragic – poor Fran, and the children of course.'

'I only knew her vaguely – slight family

connection.'

Hubert had missed his vocation in life. He should have been an actor. Today he was wearing his navy blazer and cream slacks, his 'away-day outfit', which he thought made him look a tad nautical. I thought he looked more like a 'lovey'. 'Was she a customer of yours?' he asked casually.

'She certainly was. Every Saturday morning. She came in here the morning she died. They loved entertaining. Every Saturday they had friends round for a meal. Quite informal I believe. It seems that Saturday night they cancelled. Her husband Paul said she was feeling low all day and couldn't face cooking. Strange ... she seemed the same as usual that Saturday morning.'

Rufus wrapped up the olive oil as carefully as if it were a vintage wine and when I heard the price I thought of how many bottles of cheap plonk I could buy for the same money. He also asked me if I had enjoyed the cheese. 'It was delicious,' I said. 'We'll be in again before we leave Cornwall.'

Rufus smiled, well satisfied. Hubert paid him and asked, 'Do the new owners of Tamberlake shop here?'

Rufus shook his head. 'Paul's only been in once or twice since. He was living alone for a while, although I've heard there's a new woman in his life now. He doesn't seem to have much luck with women – rather like me.' Rufus threw back his head and laughed. 'My wife lasted six months down here. Too quiet I suppose and I talk food all the time so that probably drove her away. That, and the fact she fell for a local potter. There's not that much to say about clay is there?' He laughed again. I had the feeling that Rufus was either a little mad or his laughter indicated relief that his wife had left him and he'd been a happy little soul ever since.

My energy levels were beginning to flag but Hubert, in contrast, was as bright as a hopping bunny. We sat in the car and he took out his notebook. 'One thing about small places is everybody knows everybody else. The local funeral director has been very helpful. It seems Paul was accompanied to the funeral parlour by a chap called Jamie Ingrams.'

'Have you got an address?'

Hubert nodded. 'What we really need is some police input. You could ring David, see if he'll give us a hand.'

'No way!'

'Why not?'

'He's seeing Megan and I don't want to muddy the waters.'

Hubert sighed as if I was being particularly difficult and I began to get irritated. My case was being taken over. 'I think our first priority,' I said firmly, trying to re-establish my position, 'is to see the doctor who gave evidence at the hearing.'

'I had thought of that,' he said swiftly. 'But he's not at the same practice. He's now working in Devon. So that's a journey for another day.'

Wanting to be at least one up I said, 'I want to be the one to interview him.'

Hubert looked at me closely. 'I hope you're not losing your sense of humour.'

I ignored him. The funny side of life was evading me at the moment. 'I thought I'd need a cover story, so I'll be a new, enthusiastic health visitor doing some current research into isolation and depression in women with pre-school children.'

'Sounds impressive,' said Hubert. 'You haven't lost your sense of humour then?'

I didn't respond. I was too busy thinking about how best to handle the doctor. I'd brought with me several blank identity cards and, with a passport-size photo, a decent felt-tip pen, a plastic casing, a bit of ingenuity, flat shoes, a skirt, the merest flick of lipstick and a clipboard – I would become Kate Brown, HV. I'd show Hubert who was the investigator.

Hubert drove back towards Trevelly at funereal pace to the home of Jamie Ingrams. I worried about being seen by Helen so I kept my head down just in case. After all, she'd managed to spot me in Wales and if she saw me now it could ruin everything. Hubert glanced at me as I hunched down in the front seat. He had a plan it seemed. 'We're police officers from the Met, investigating the disappearance of Paul Warrinder's former girlfriend,' he said. 'What did you say her name was?'

'I didn't. Hang on, I'll try to think.'

I found it worrying that I'd forgotten her name. Eventually I came up with 'Alison' and the 'Peters' soon followed. 'What do we know about her?' asked Hubert.

'Nothing. Just that she got as far as the wedding dress and then they broke up and she...'

I broke off, annoyed with myself for not knowing more. Hubert became conciliatory.

'You can't find out everything in a few days. That's what we're here for.'

'We don't know for sure she's actually *"disappeared"*. If he jilted her she's not going to be sending him postcards is she?' Hubert nodded and even managed to speed up a little.

I sat watching the countryside pass by. Summer was ending and the trees and fields had a parched and jaded look. Tamberlake had that jaded look too but it would have no regeneration in the spring. Two young women had had their moments of happiness there but how abruptly that had changed. Was Paul evil? Or was it the house itself? Surely in five years Fran would have known most of Paul's secrets, or at least what she'd found out that Saturday wouldn't have come as too great a shock. Sometimes the simple answers are the only answers. He was a very attractive man. Maybe he wouldn't cheat in his own back yard, but if for both women a revelation about another woman had come as a terrible shock, who knows what sort of emotional reaction there could have been. Did Helen have some inkling that he was cheating on her? Was that the cause of her anxiety? Mere suspicion but enough to blight anyone's wedding day. When he was at Tamberlake she could relax because she knew exactly where he was. And surely no woman could tolerate a locked room? And was she lying about not having a key to the attic room?

'You all right?' asked Hubert.

'Fine. Just thinking.'

'Well don't start fretting and jumping to conclusions. We've got to keep an open mind.'

'Thank you – oh wise one – I'm the investigator not you.'

'That's it, Kate – you get the bit between your teeth. This could be your finest hour.'

Somehow I doubted that but I muttered, 'Yeah, yeah.'

Jamie Ingrams lived on the first floor of a three-storey block of flats overlooking a park. He answered the entry phone so quickly that it was as if he was expecting us.

'Police?' he enquired. We nodded with supreme confidence. Hubert introduced himself as DCI Rodney Stone and me as DI Cheryl West. Why Hubert had decided to call himself Rodney was beyond me but I supposed it was an improvement on Hubert.

Jamie was jockey-height and boyishly slim. He looked at first glance to be in his twenties but on closer inspection he had lines around his eyes and slightly receding floppy fair hair. He was probably in his late thirties. In old age he would be gnome-like.

The apartment suited his size and Hubert and I, standing, constituted a crowd. Jamie had made attempts to make the flat look bigger by mirrors and pure white walls and small black furniture. There was no clutter and no sign of hobbies. There was an arrangement of bright geometric prints on one wall adding to the modern feel. I tried to guess his occupation but couldn't. Judging from his flat he didn't bring work home.

'You've come about Alison haven't you?' he asked as he directed us to sit down. We nodded. 'Good. I'm glad the police have taken notice at last.'

'Would you like to explain that, sir?' When Hubert acted 'cop' he seemed to model his behaviour on old black and white movies. He talked slowly and enunciated every word as if he were dealing with the dull-witted.

Not that Jamie seemed to notice. He was keen to talk. 'I'd given up on anyone taking any sort of action. She's been missing now for more than six years. I've tried to find her but the local police said they couldn't help me because she was an adult and, although they were sympathetic, they said they simply hadn't got the manpower.'

'Would you like to start from the beginning, sir?' said Hubert, flicking open his notebook. 'What exactly was your connection with Alison Peters?'

Jamie looked slightly surprised, as if Hubert should have known. Then he glanced at me, as if with momentary suspicion. 'She's my sister,' he said. 'Well, half-sister.'

Eleven

Hubert and I tried to keep impassive expressions.

'I introduced her to Paul,' said Jamie. 'He was a long-term friend of mine and I thought they'd get on. Alison worked in London as a fashion buyer for one of the chain stores. She loved her job but she fell for Paul, gave it up and moved into Tamberlake – all in the space of two months.'

'You didn't feel happy about the relationship?' I asked.

He shrugged. 'I was fairly neutral, I just thought it was rushed. When they started to make wedding plans, I'll admit I wasn't too pleased at first.'

'Did you have doubts about Paul Warrinder?'

Jamie shook his head. 'I could see the attraction, he's a good-looking guy and he owned Tamberlake. Alison liked the finer things of life, designer clothes, holidays abroad, good food and wine. I think she thought Paul was a good marital bet, which

I suppose he was. I thought so too at the time...'

'But you don't anymore?'

'I had reservations. I was a great deal more upset when he married Fran less than six months after Alison left Tamberlake.'

'Did you know Fran?' asked Hubert.

'Oh yes. She was a lovely girl.'

'So you remained on good terms with Paul?'

Jamie looked sharply at Hubert. 'Are you saying I shouldn't have? He didn't jilt my sister. She decided he just couldn't offer her enough. His income was a bit erratic and I think she just got cold feet about the wedding.'

'Did she tell you that?'

'Not in so many words. She was cold ... you know. Chilled.'

'Were you close?' I asked.

He shook his head. 'No, we were never really close. We kept in touch and my mother's death brought us closer. She died of alcohol poisoning when Alison was twenty. Our respective fathers had long since abandoned us. So in effect there are only Alison and I. And since I haven't heard from Alison in six years something may well have happened to her.'

'I'm sorry to ask this question,' I said, 'but it is my job.'

He smiled at me briefly.

'Did your sister have any money?'

'Oh yes. Our mother left us a substantial house, not quite Tamberlake but in the South of England, and some capital. Mother had family money which, had she lived to old age, she'd have pissed it all away. I bought this flat and invested the rest of the money. It means I only take temporary jobs as the fancy takes me. I'm basically an idle bastard.'

Strange, I thought, how often some people never answer the question you actually asked.

Hubert gave a little smug nod in my direction.

'And Alison's share?' I persisted.

'That's the strange part,' he said, frowning. 'She's spent quite a bit enjoying herself, travelling, not working, that sort of thing. But two weeks before she left I met her quite by accident coming out of the bank. She'd closed her high-interest accounts and said she'd left just a couple of thousand in her current account. When I asked her why, she told me to mind my own business but I wasn't to tell Paul. All would be revealed later. Well I'm still waiting.'

'She sounds the impulsive type,' I suggested.

'She was *that* all right. She followed her whims. Maybe Paul fell into that category, I don't know. I think that she planned to go abroad and spend her money recklessly. I wasn't that worried in the first year. She wasn't much of a communicator. But she did send Christmas cards – always. And when someone doesn't send a Christmas card for six years you begin to doubt they are still alive.'

'What about...' I began but he held up a hand to silence me.

'What about tea or coffee? I'm parched.'

'Lovely. Thank you.'

He walked the few yards to the kitchen and closed the door and I didn't hear any tap running or cups rattling. 'Go and check on him, Hubert, I think he's phoning someone.'

Hubert didn't look too pleased – 'Yes, ma'am,' he said, saluting me. He came back seconds later to tell me that Jamie was indeed making a call.

A tray of coffee and biscuits eventually arrived. Jamie played mother and handed me a cup and saucer. 'Now then, Jamie,' I said, feeling clumsy holding delicate china in one hand and a biscuit in the other. 'What about Paul's reaction to Alison leaving. How much did he know about her plans?'

He paused for a moment and I felt he was carefully considering his answer.

'It came as a great shock to him of course. He looked ill that day, he was really upset. He said he'd been given no warning. She was leaving because she didn't feel ready to settle down.'

He sipped at his coffee for a few moments and then Hubert said bluntly, 'So, you're pretty sure Alison is dead?'

There was a short pause before he said sadly, 'Yes. It's just a gut feeling.'

'And who do you think killed her, sir?'

Jamie looked flummoxed. 'I hadn't thought about that. I mean, who ... She probably died in some third-world country ... an accident.'

'There would still have been a body, sir, third world or not.'

'Yes. You're right.'

'What about sightings, sir?'

'What do you mean?'

'Did anyone see her leave Tamberlake or get on a train or board a plane?'

'Not that I know of. She left fairly late. That might have been on impulse.'

'I see, sir,' said Hubert slowly. 'So it seems the last person to see Alison was in fact Paul Warrinder. Do you think he tried to persuade her not to leave?'

'What are you suggesting? That Paul had something to do with her disappearance? That's ridiculous. He was upset but he wasn't angry. Anyway he's not the violent type. I've known him for years.'

'I'm merely making enquiries, sir. Could we talk about Fran now?'

Jamie refilled his coffee cup and sat down.

'Can you make this quick?' he said. 'It's very painful. What I can tell you is he met Fran in a wine bar. I was there and I have to say she looked like Alison – same physical type. Six months later they were married.'

'Did she move into Tamberlake before she got married?'

'No. Afterwards.'

'Did she like the house?'

'She thought the house had bad vibes but she got used to it. She was pregnant soon after getting married and Paul didn't think a major upheaval would be good for her.'

'So you saw them quite often?'

'Yeah. Usually once a week. Saturday nights Paul would invite people. Fran did the shopping and Paul did the cooking. Simple stuff, spag bol, chilli, curries. Big-bowl stuff. But we had good wine with the meal – it was great.'

'And when the children came along – you still saw them on Saturday nights?'

'Yes. The kids were in bed. They were good sleepers.'

'And Fran coped when Paul was away?'

'She had a cleaning lady three times a week.'

'We'll need her name and address. And any friends or relatives or anyone who could shed light on Alison's whereabouts.'

He shook his head. 'No, I've asked around. The cleaner's name is Carole Jackson.

Number four Robin Crescent. It's just around the corner.' Hubert wrote down the address in his careful hand as Jamie scrawled down some names and addresses on the back of an envelope. 'I have contacted these people,' said Jamie defensively. 'But obviously with no result.'

Hubert was on another tack by now. 'So, Warrinder didn't have any money problems,' he muttered, as if to himself. 'They entertained, had a cleaning lady. Gardener?'

'Bill Andrews did the garden. He still does a bit occasionally. He's well over seventy.'

'So who paid for all this?'

Jamie looked a bit taken aback by Hubert's bluntness. 'Fran took care of the gardener and the cleaner. Paul paid all the utilities.'

'Fran had money too then?'

Jamie looked daggers at Hubert. 'You're at it again. Innuendo. Money attracts money. She had a pile of elderly relatives who seemed to die one after the other, so, yes, she did have her own money. But she didn't brag about it. She had modest tastes – she was the artistic type. She'd been to art school. I believe she'd sold a few watercolours. Fran didn't need to do nine to five to survive...' He broke off at the word 'survive', as if realizing maybe she hadn't in fact survived.

I took over again, deciding to change the subject. 'What if I were to tell you that at this moment Paul is pretending to be in

Argentina?'

Jamie looked at me sharply. 'What are you talking about?'

'I'm telling you Paul Warrinder has told Helen that he is in Argentina when he isn't.'

'Well where is he then?'

'I thought perhaps you could tell me. Shall I tell you what we suspect?'

'Go ahead,' he said, obviously rattled. 'It's bound to be ridiculous.'

'I think he has another woman.'

Jamie threw back his head and laughed. 'Not Paul. You really are barking up the wrong tree. He's a one-woman man. Always has been.'

'How can you be so sure?'

'I just know, that's all.'

I decided to drop that point for the moment. 'Nearly finished with the questions,' I said soothingly. 'I'd just like to clarify what happened on the Saturday that Fran and the children died.'

He looked at me with slight suspicion. 'I thought you were here about my half-sister, after all, she's the one who seems to have disappeared. Fran's death was tragic but there was no mystery about it. I blame the doctor.'

'Why's that?'

'He prescribed those pills for her.'

'What were they for?'

'He said at the inquest that she was

131

depressed and had trouble sleeping. It was those pills she gave the children and took herself.'

'He obviously treated her in good faith.'

'She never seemed depressed to me.'

'Perhaps she put on a cheerful front.'

He frowned, unconvinced.

'Maybe,' I said, 'she didn't appear depressed, because the medication *did work*.'

'Why then did she kill herself and those poor kids?' His voice cracked slightly. It struck me that he was more upset about Fran and the children than he was about the presumed death of his half-sister.

'You were fond of the children?'

'I love kids. And those two were great. I used to babysit from when they were born. Fran knew she could always rely on me to take care of them. Why did the silly cow...' He broke off. 'It upsets me.'

He still hadn't answered my question about that Saturday night. 'Have you any idea why Fran cancelled the dinner party? She did the shopping for it and then suddenly it was all off. Did Paul ring you to tell you?'

There was a slight pause before he answered. 'Yeah, he rang to say she was off-colour – nothing specific.'

'What time was that?'

'Afternoon, about four. I can't really remember the exact time.'

'Were you surprised?'

'Not really.'

Although I hadn't asked any difficult questions he continued to look vaguely uncomfortable, like a man losing a fight and expecting the next blow. 'What does surprise me,' I said – he looked at me expectantly – 'is that Fran didn't leave a note. By not leaving one it must have been especially hurtful for Paul. After all, no one seems to have any idea why she did it.'

He nodded as if in agreement.

'Your half-sister, just as abruptly, takes back her wedding dress and runs off. To me that smacks of Paul being responsible.'

'You're talking bloody nonsense. What on earth would Paul have done to make them unhappy? He loved them both, and his kids.'

'Are you so sure of that?'

'I can only speak as I find. Paul is...' He paused and in that moment I knew exactly his dilemma. 'I'm...'

'You're in love with him.'

Twelve

After a few minutes Hubert drove away from Jamie Ingrams's flat and parked round the corner. I sensed he was a little peeved that I'd found out something he hadn't thought of but being curious he had to ask. 'The only reason I guessed Jamie was in love with Paul,' I said, 'and I know it sounds corny, but his eyes lit up at the sound of his name.'

Hubert muttered that he'd thought Jamie was in love with Fran.

'I'm sure he was fond of her but it was Paul he wanted.'

'But Paul isn't gay?' asked Hubert, sounding somewhat confused.

'Jamie only claimed unrequited love. Paul *could* be bisexual but he obviously didn't fancy Jamie.'

'Where does that get us then?' asked Hubert dejectedly.

'Back to the hotel, dinner and then bed, I hope.'

'That's your trouble, Kate, creature comforts, that's all you want.'

'Not quite,' I said, hoping to sound less of

a hedonist. 'There are more important things in life than food and bed.'

'Name two,' said Hubert, smirking. 'And don't say sex, because you don't get any.'

'The pursuit of truth is one,' I said haughtily. Hubert laughed until he grew pink in the face. 'You'll see,' I snapped. 'Forget comfort, let's go and see the cleaning lady now.'

Carole Jackson lived around the next corner in a small semi. Hubert, living in yesteryear, expected an apron and a mop and bucket. Instead, the woman who answered the door wore embroidered jeans, a skimpy top and high heeled mules. She was perhaps forty but she was living proof that the forties *are* the new thirties. Her make-up was immaculate and her nails, improbably long for the real thing, were multi-coloured. I did the introductions, Stone and West, because Hubert seemed a little preoccupied with her feet. Carole had one of those voices that would calm a knife-wielding maniac, and angelic features that, if recovering from anaesthesia, would immediately be a comfort. Hubert became incapable of speech and as she guided us through to her living room I jabbed him in the back with my finger. That seemed to bring him to, because he flashed me an angry look as if I'd wrecked one of his best erotic moments. Which I probably had.

Our visit didn't seem to come as a surprise.

'Have you come about Alison?' she asked.

'Alison *and* Fran.'

'You sit down. I've got plenty of time. Last time I saw the police they rushed me. Short of manpower they said they were.'

We sat down on a two-seater sofa while Carole sat on a window seat. Hubert was still mesmerized, so much so that I had to explain, 'DCI Stone is the strong silent type. But we've got plenty of time too and we thought you might be able to help us.'

'I'll do my best. I think about what happened over and over. Sometimes I think if I think about it long enough I'll make sense of it.'

'How do you mean?'

'Little things I keep remembering, but sometimes my memory plays tricks, after all, it was a long time ago now.'

'Give me an example.'

She thought for a moment. 'All right. I used to clean for Alison on Mondays, Wednesdays and Fridays from ten till four. She was ever so excited about her wedding. On that Saturday in June she went to pick up her dress. She even rang me to tell me how thrilled she was with the dress. Then when I came on Monday she was so quiet that I asked her what was wrong. I thought her and Paul had had a row but she said no and she didn't want to talk about it. At the time I thought it was because Paul had gone abroad that day and she was missing him. But now...'

'Now?'

'It's only a feeling if you know what I mean and I don't like to speak ill of anyone, especially when he seemed so heartbroken when she left, but...'

'You can tell me.'

'Yeah. You're right. It's best if I tell you,' she said. 'It was after she took the dress back that she made one or two comments about Paul. She said more to me on the Wednesday. He'd gone abroad by then and he'd be away for a week. She seemed a bit more cheerful; perhaps it was relief he wasn't in the house. She said that she didn't know him well enough to marry him and at first I thought she was planning to carry on living at Tamberlake, just staying single. But I was wrong about that. Alison was a private sort of person, a bit reserved, but I can see now that it could have been something else.'

'What exactly?'

'Fear. She was afraid of him. Too afraid to tell him she'd taken the dress back and the wedding was off.'

'Most women would baulk at telling a man news like that.'

'No,' said Carole firmly. 'It was more than that. She *had* to get away from him.'

'When did she give him the news the wedding was off?'

'I don't know. At first she'd seemed sort of relieved but the Friday of that week she closed down on me. Before that time she used to work alongside me in the house and we used to chat about everything. We were very different: she'd had a nice middle-class upbringing, I brought three sisters and myself up with no mother and a work-shy father. But we both liked to laugh...' She broke off suddenly and said very quietly, 'She's dead, isn't she?'

Hubert, managing to take his eyes from her feet, suddenly said, 'Do you think Paul killed her?'

'He couldn't have. He wasn't in the country. He was abroad somewhere – Argentina, I think.'

'But if he wasn't in Argentina?'

Carole uncrossed her legs. 'Alison never told me he was violent. She *was* in love with him. But I think he had secrets.'

'Most men have a few secrets,' said Hubert.

'I know that,' said Carole. 'I've been married – to a real bastard. He was a bit like Paul, good-looking; he could charm me with a handful of words. I thought he was wonderful too until the day he kicked me down the stairs and carried on kicking me as I lay at the bottom. He left me there. I lay for three hours before a neighbour looked through the letterbox and saw me. I was two weeks in hospital. He'd ruptured my spleen. I never saw him again. I don't expect the police are trying too hard to find him. Much the same as with Alison.'

Silence fell on us.

She'd told us in such a matter of fact way that it had a subduing effect on both Hubert and me.

'I'll make some tea,' she said, as if she sensed we all needed something other than pure realism. She walked out of the room, leaving us silent and Hubert looking pensive.

'What are you thinking?' he asked.

'I dunno. I was just thinking if he had killed her out of pique there's no body and how could anyone prove he *had* killed her. Too much time has gone by.'

'Don't be defeatist, Kate. Remember that today you're a DI. I don't think he killed her because she wouldn't marry him. I think he would have taken that on the chin. His friends would have rallied round...'

'What did you say?' I interrupted.

Hubert looked mystified. 'His friends would have rallied round,' he repeated.

'Don't you see?' I said, trying to contain my excitement. '*His* friends – not hers...' I broke off as Carole came in with a tray of tea and cake.

The arrival of nourishment halted my train of thought. The fruitcake was home-made. Carole didn't eat any and neither did Hubert but I managed some. Carole sipped her tea thoughtfully and then without being prompted carried on talking. It was as if, at long last, she had her chance to tell the story. 'I came in on Monday morning,' she said. 'It was a lovely bright morning. I let myself in with the key and called out to her. It was so quiet. I knew immediately the house was empty. I checked her wardrobes. They were empty. Then I went down to the kitchen to look for a note, maybe a forwarding address. There was nothing ... except it was obvious she'd had the usual Saturday night meal. I checked the fridge. Normally there'd be enough fresh food for at least six people but judging from leftovers they hadn't eaten as much as usual. There was something odd though ... an envelope with my name on had fallen under the kitchen table. There was nothing inside. It was as if she was going to leave me something and had been interrupted.'

'What did you do with the envelope?'

'Nothing, I left it on the table. Paul was due home that afternoon. So I did my usual cleaning. Got rid of the rubbish, mopped the floors and polished and vacuumed the carpets. Paul arrived back at about two o'clock. I had to tell him Alison had taken all her clothes, belongings ... and gone.'

'How did he take it?'

Carole shrugged. 'Silently. Then after a few

140

minutes he asked if she'd left a note. I just pointed to the empty envelope. He screwed that up and then said he was going up to the attic. I asked him if he wanted me to do my usual hours and he just nodded.'

'When you say belongings – what did you mean? Lamps, radio, CD collection?'

'Oh no, just a couple of suitcases, I think.'

'Did she take her car?'

'Must have done. It wasn't in the garage.'

'Carole, you say Alison was frightened of Paul for some reason. Could that explain why she's never been in touch?'

Carole thought for a moment. 'She would have rung me on my mobile ... if she could ... just to say cheerio.'

'What about her friends?'

'I know some of them. I thought her half-brother Jamie might know but he denied knowing anything about her plans. He said he was there on that Saturday night and she'd seemed perfectly normal. Her girl-friends didn't even know she'd sent the wedding dress back.'

'Did anyone report her missing?'

'No. Not that I know of. Jamie got con-cerned after about a year with no word but he said she'd probably gone abroad.'

'Did you tell the local police about your suspicions?'

'I didn't really get a chance. It must have been two years later when a constable asked me a few questions but, as I said, he didn't have the time.'

'And was it different when Fran died?'

'Yes. They asked more questions but they said it was obvious that due to the "balance of her mind" she'd committed suicide and taken the children with her.'

'You were still working three days a week at Tamberlake?'

'Yes.'

'And what did you think of Fran's state of mind? At the inquest Paul said she was depressed, her doctor mentioned depression. What did you think?'

Carole finished her tea and placed the cup and saucer carefully back on the tray. Hubert by my side was busily taking notes and keeping a low profile. 'She was a great mum, always cheerful around the kids. They were so bonnie ... poor little mites. Charlotte was three, a real little chatterbox and very active. Always running and climbing and Josh was eighteen months, chubby and placid and bright as a button. As I said, when I was there she always seemed perfectly normal. I know she found being alone in the house difficult, especially when Paul was away. She asked me once to come in every day but I had other job commitments and so I turned her down. I wish I hadn't now.'

'Did you think *she* was frightened of Paul?'

'Oh no. She was frightened of the house.

She was convinced it was haunted. She had trouble sleeping at night. Charlotte and Josh usually slept well but she did say on the day before she died that Josh was teething and she'd crept in beside Charlotte so that she could soothe him. The children shared a bedroom and when Paul was away she told me they all piled into the one bed.'

'Did she see ghosts or hear them?'

'No, it was odd. She said she could hear the sea as though there was a storm blowing but when she went outside she couldn't hear it. Sometimes she'd walk a little way down the path until she could see the sea, just to confirm there was no storm.'

'This was late at night?'

'Yes. I told the police but Paul denied she ever left the house at night while he was there.'

'How did he explain the fact that she'd left the house that Saturday night?'

'His excuse was he was so drunk he didn't know that she'd left the house. The police took blood samples and he still had high levels of alcohol. So that was that. The verdict was that she'd given the children some of her crushed-up tablets, taken some herself and walked out into the night and had gone over the cliff edge.'

Hubert cleared his throat as if to tell me he wanted his share of the questions.

'What type of people are these friends of

Paul?' he asked.

Carole shrugged. 'Not my type, that's for sure. A bit trendy. Young, rich and with no kids. Dead shallow. Not the sort you'd go to if you were in trouble. If it would help, I've got one or two photos of them round the table. The light in the kitchen isn't that good but they always ate in the kitchen.'

She produced a photo album and eventually found two photos of a group of six people looking slightly jaded around a candlelit table with the remains of a meal in front of them. Carole pointed them out one by one. I was surprised when she told me she had their addresses. 'I know I shouldn't have done it but after about four months Paul decided to get rid of everything that belonged to Fran and the kids. Everything. He didn't even want to keep photos. He said I could have anything I wanted. I took her address book, I don't know why. At first I thought it was her diary but that had gone missing. I knew she kept a diary but Paul said the police must have lost it ... I didn't believe that.'

'Could we borrow the address book?'

'Yeah, I'll get it for you.'

She left the room and returned seconds later with a fabric-covered address book. 'I don't think he contacted everyone in here,' she said as she handed it to me. 'There were very few at the funeral.'

144

'Cremation?' queried Hubert.

She nodded.

Hubert glanced at his watch and stood up. It was time to go. Even Hubert doesn't like to miss a meal he's paid for.

'There is something else ... it's about the night she died.'

Strange, I thought, how often people leave the crux of a matter until last. 'The police asked me at the time if I knew why Fran had cancelled that Saturday night dinner with their friends. I was upset and told them that I had no idea, which was true. On the Monday I came in as usual but the police were milling around. They told me I could carry on as usual. I took the vacuum bag outside to empty in the wheelie bin. There was a black bag open on the top, I could easily see three of those polystyrene trays, several empty wine bottles and a plastic bag from the deli.'

'What did that tell you?'

She glanced at me as if I was dim. 'Those bits of packaging and leftovers told me that Paul hadn't cancelled the Saturday night dinner party. It *had* gone ahead. So he'd lied to the police. And why would he do that?'

'Why indeed?' I said.

Thirteen

Hubert sighed as we left Carole's house. 'I'm not feeling that good,' he said. His face did look pale and I thought he'd overstretched himself with the journey and the visits. I knew he wasn't exaggerating when he allowed me to drive the car back to the Regis Hotel. We arrived as the first diners were being served. Hubert rushed to his room to let Jasper out for a run in the garden. He reported back that Jasper was sulking and that we should take him with us tomorrow. I promised to take him for a long walk later and I ordered two double brandies simply because I thought we both needed and deserved them. Hubert perked up during the meal and luckily we were sat at a corner table where we could talk privately.

'We need police help on this one,' he said.

I sat for a while staring at a piece of spinach that was decorating his front teeth.

'You're not listening to me, are you?' he said. 'What did I just say?'

'We need police help? They haven't been exactly competent so far, have they?'

'You don't listen, do you? I also said that we should get in touch with the "key" man, Robert Roberts. He's ex-police, isn't he?'

I nodded. 'You've got spinach stuck to your front teeth.'

Hubert scowled and left the dining room. I sat watching the other diners but wasn't really observing them. What consumed me at the moment was why Paul should lie so blatantly. Why not tell the police they did have friends round that night? Maybe, I thought, because the police would have interviewed them and he wanted to protect them, for, after all, they knew nothing of Fran's early-morning walk to her death? Or did they? I remembered Hubert's words – 'his friends would have rallied round him'. Rallied, lied or just kept quiet? Either way there was some sort of cover-up. And I would need to talk to Carole again. Why did she no longer work at Tamberlake? Did she know too much?

Hubert returned to the table and bared spinach-free gnashers. 'Does that suit madam?' he asked.

'Don't be childish.'

The dessert trolley appeared then and after much deliberation Hubert chose fresh fruit salad and I chose strawberry torte. My motto for eating out is to rarely choose anything you can either cook or prepare for yourself. Strawberry torte was not in my culinary repertoire. I was halfway through and 'oohing' and 'aahing' at how delicious it was when my mobile rang. It was Gill. I hadn't given Gill or Helen a thought all day and wasn't quite sure how much I should tell her.

'I haven't got long,' she said, sounding breathless. 'Helen's in the bath. Where are you?'

'The Regis Hotel.'

'Paul's back in a couple of days. Supposedly ringing from Argentina. If you want access to the house, tomorrow would be good, we're still searching for the "going-away" outfit.'

'What time?'

'Eleven. I want to see you before I go, Kate. I'll ring you and let you know when.'

'OK. Do you know where the hotel is?'

'I'll find it. I've got to go now. Be careful.'

On that cryptic note she was gone. My strawberry torte lay splayed in front of me, less inviting now, the decorative strawberry on top squashed and as red as blood. I pushed the plate away.

'What's up?' asked Hubert. 'You don't leave desserts.'

'I'm full up,' I said, not wanting to elaborate.

'It's not like you,' he said. 'I'm worried. I'm off to bed before you expire from calorie deficit.'

I had one more drink in the bar, sitting alone on a chesterfield sofa and sipping at a brandy and soda. But not for long. A chubby man with glasses and a shiny pate sat beside me. 'You on holiday, love?'

'No,' I snapped. 'Murder enquiry.' He moved away so fast he nearly fell over. To help me look occupied and keep strange older men away I pulled out from my handbag the two photos that Carole had given me. I was trying to memorize their faces in case I saw any of them out and about. I guessed that Paul had taken one of the photographs and Fran the other. Paul was smiling and looking relaxed and as handsome as ever, although in the candlelight he seemed to have some designer stubble. That could have been due to the poor light. Fran was smiling but it looked false, or was I imagining that, knowing how short her life would be?

I finished my drink unaccosted by any other man, felt vaguely disappointed about that and strangely wide awake. I crept into Hubert's room to collect Jasper and we walked out into the night together. It was dark but the air was still and warm. Even so it smelt of autumn and I felt a little sad that summer would soon end.

Walking a dog at night when few people are around is a joy. You can talk and not be overheard and also not feel as if you're verging on dementia by talking totally to yourself. I put the facts to Jasper and he gave one of his quick yaps, so I take it he approved.

We walked out of the hotel car park and along a track that led eventually to a small row of cottages faced only by a bank of bushes. Most residents had their lights on and no net curtains, so I took surreptitious glances at their décor. Jasper, though, wanted to pee against their gates, so I had no time to linger and at the end of the row we turned back towards the hotel.

There were several cars in the car park. Jasper had paused for yet another sniffing session and I noticed two men in a black car talking animatedly. It was the smaller man in the driving seat I recognized – small head, floppy fair hair – Jamie. Next to him sat Paul! I yanked poor Jasper away so fast his feet hardly touched the ground. Once in the foyer of the hotel I picked Jasper up, tucked him under my arm and ran to Hubert's room and plonked him on the floor. Hubert didn't stir but his car keys had been placed neatly by his loose change on his bedside table. I grabbed the car keys and rushed out. As I got to the car park, they were just leaving. Luckily they wanted to do a right turn and the late-night traffic was building up, so I had a chance to be ready as soon as they managed to exit.

Unfortunately my night driving can be readily compared to an elderly male Sunday driver wearing a cap. My sense of direction is so poor as to be comparable with someone who has undergone a prolonged period of sensory deprivation. I wasn't sure if we were making for Jamie's place or Tamberlake but I kept behind at a safe distance and followed the tail lights.

Mile after mile swiftly passed by. The village names barely registered as I concentrated on keeping up with Jamie.

Eventually he turned left off the main road into a narrow lane. Since I was the only car behind him he'd soon realize he was being followed, so at the first widening of the lane I stopped and waited for a few minutes. When he was out of sight I drove on.

And on and on, to a village called Great Marrington where the car seemed to disappear. I drove on through the village, which did boast a well-lit pub and two street lamps. I was about to give up and go back to the hotel when I glimpsed two men at a chalet-style house, the last in the village, set a hundred yards or so back from any other house. It was built high up with two sets of stone steps to get to the front door. All the curtains were drawn and Jamie and Paul were already going inside the house. Irritatingly I caught only a glimpse of the person at the door, who appeared to be male with dark hair.

I waited in a lay-by watching the house. It was now eleven thirty and maybe they wouldn't stay long. That was the theory. I dozed for a while and then at one a.m. the house lights went out. There was no reason for me to stay now; they were obviously staying the night.

Although I seemed to be following the same route back I found it nerve-wracking in the dark and I made one or two wrong turns, so the journey back took more than an hour. The sight of the Regis Hotel was the best thing I'd seen all day.

Even though it was after two a.m. I still had one more job to do. I rang Gill, who was half-dopey with sleep, so I kept my message to a minimum – Paul was back in Cornwall but seemed in no rush to be with his fiancée.

In the morning a perky Hubert came to wake me. It was only seven thirty and already he'd taken Jasper for a long walk. My eyes refused to open properly and I felt as if I'd aged five years in as many hours. A shower and two cups of tea later I felt ready to face breakfast and the day ahead.

I told Hubert about my tailing Jamie and Paul and the fact that it hadn't achieved much. 'I wonder why he's taking such a chance?' muttered Hubert. 'You saw him, others may see him. More to the point, has Jamie checked us out and found Stone and

West do not exist?'

'If it's not sex it must be money,' I suggested. Hubert merely chewed on his toast thoughtfully.

'What do you think our priority is today?' I asked. 'Because Gill is taking Helen out shopping, leaving the house empty, and we could have a really good look round.'

'What time?'

'Eleven.'

'We'd better make sure Paul isn't hanging around and before we go there I want to speak to Robert Roberts – he may have contacts.'

Hubert insisted that we take Jasper and by nine we were on our way to see the ex-cop turned locksmith.

Robert Roberts lived in a detached bungalow about four miles north of Trevelly. As we drove up he was painting his garage door. He turned and peered at us and when I told him I was a private investigator his expression registered a mixture of surprise and pity. 'Got your work cut out on this one then,' he said. 'Talk about a cocked-up investigation. Modern police work these days is all bloody paperwork and worrying about procedure and human rights. In my day Warrinder would have been worked over until he confessed.'

'So you think he's guilty then?' I asked.

'Guilty as bloody sin.'

'What of?'

He stared at my head, needing no words, he had already decided I was brainless.

'Come on in the house,' he said. 'I'm ready for a cuppa. Let the dog out, he can have the run of the garden.' Jasper, released from the car, tore twice around the garden and then began sniffing individual plants and bushes. I knew he'd pee on most of them but I doubted it would do them much harm.

Once inside the bungalow Hubert paid Roberts a compliment about his conservatory extension and Roberts responded by offering Hubert a guided tour. I was left in the lounge to stare at the Spanish-style furnishings, marble-tiled floors and terracotta walls. There were even two sombreros and a pair of castanets on the walls, which I thought was a little OTT.

When eventually they returned, still deep in conversation about grouting and varieties of wood panelling, I felt a little superfluous, although Hubert did wink at me. I knew damn well he wasn't in the least bit interested in DIY, so I guessed that he had some sort of plan.

Roberts went off to make the tea, giving me a chance to ask Hubert what he was up to.

'He's originally from just outside Longborough.'

'So?'

'So, he's got several very elderly relatives.'
My mouth dropped. 'I'm gobsmacked! You're drumming up custom and I've been sitting here like a ... constipated prune!'

Hubert merely laughed. 'Well you're not a dried up old prune ... yet.'

I didn't feel in the slightest bit mollified but when Roberts came into the living room with a tray of mugs, he wasn't alone. Beside him was a tall good-looking thirty-something man with a wide smile, wearing only shorts and a six pack. 'This is my son – Liam. He's a DS but soon to make DI.'

Hubert moved forward and shook hands with him. Liam then walked across to me and bent down to shake my hand. 'Hi, Kate. It is Kate, isn't it?' I nodded. I couldn't quite find my voice, because I'd looked into his eyes and they were the deepest of blues and for those few moments I was lost. It was of course lust at first sight and it was sure to be unrequited lust, so I took a deep breath and told myself to get a grip. He'd come as a real surprise. I was convinced he was adopted because he bore no resemblance to Roberts senior. He was several inches taller; his features were rugged whereas his father's were somewhat flat.

I think Hubert may have noticed I was preoccupied, because he turned to Roberts senior and said, 'We'd be grateful for any help on this case. One of Kate's old school

155

friends is planning to marry Warrinder in a few weeks and her bridesmaid to be – Gill – is very concerned.'

'I'm not surprised. I've met Gill. I made the key for her, partly so I could have another look round the place. He's a cocky bastard. He's got away with murder. I know he has.'

Liam picked up a mug of coffee and handed one to Hubert and the other to me and, much to my surprise, sat next to me. It was only a two-seater sofa and, as we were forced to sit so close together, his thigh was touching mine and I could smell his fresh male sweat. If I'd been wearing a corset I would have had a panic attack. My brain just seemed to close down and I had to struggle to listen to what Roberts senior was saying.

'I was a DS when Alison went missing. Not that she was reported missing until she'd been gone for more than a year. One or two basic enquiries were made but it seems she'd been planning to go, taking money out of her bank accounts some days before. She took her belongings and her car and the thinking was that if she'd wanted anyone to know where she was she would have contacted them.'

'And is that what you thought?'

'No. And I never will. Warrinder killed her or got someone else to do it, but with no body and no back-up there was nothing else

I could do. The superintendent, one of those graduate fast-trackers, was good at moving paper and charming the chief constable, but he didn't know his arse from his elbow and he gave us no bloody support.'

'What about motive?' I asked.

'Money,' he said. 'She had cash. Quite a lot. We made a few basic enquiries when we were eventually alerted but there was no trace of her or her money. She had new credit cards that were never used. Now, you tell me of a woman with new credit cards who doesn't use them.' He didn't give me a chance to refute that. 'She's dead, I tell you. Only death stops a woman spending.'

Hubert sat nodding in agreement and Liam whispered in my ear. 'My mother liked spending, he's biased.'

'Is she...?'

'No she's not in the shopping mall in the sky. She's in Devon spending her new husband's money.'

'I'm sorry,' I murmured, not being able to think of anything appropriate.

'Don't be sorry. I still see her. Dad's grateful his pension isn't being frittered away and the new husband has so much money he's delighted to have a new wife to spend it for him.'

It's true, I thought, there is 'nowt as queer as folk'. But even thinking that, to me Liam seemed normal enough, and at that moment

I was prepared to believe he was a virtual saint. Lust is addling your brain, my inner nag murmured to me but I knew given the slightest opportunity I'd be struck deaf.

'Kate, are you listening? Robert's got something to say about Fran's death.' Robert looked across at us. 'Liam, save your comments for later. Kate's around here for a few days.'

'OK, OK. I'll tell her the family secrets in private.'

Robert didn't look pleased at that comment but I think it was more that he wanted to expound his views rather than watch his son flirting with me. 'The investigation was slipshod...' he began. 'It was a total farce. In his statement Warrinder said he woke at eight thirty a.m. Fran wasn't in the bed beside him, so he presumed she was with the children. He went downstairs and there was no evidence of them having had breakfast, and the double buggy was gone, so he assumed they'd gone for an early morning walk. It seems she liked to be out of the house at every opportunity. It was a lovely morning so he wasn't surprised or worried that she'd gone out. He had a leisurely breakfast and it was nine thirty before he decided to go and look for them. He said he walked down to the beach, there was no sign of them there, then he came back up from the beach and took the cliff-top path. After that he came straight home and phoned the police.'

'It sounds plausible so far,' I said.

Roberts turned to Hubert. 'What do you think?'

Hubert frowned. 'So far I can't see what else he could have done. What did the police do?'

'That's where I think it went pear-shaped. Warrinder rang the local police in Trevelly. It's a police house, blue light outside, police constable inside with a wife and two kids. He's not overworked. The odd scrap to sort out on a Saturday night, a bit of low-grade nicking, the odd car being taken for a joyride. Anyway, Warrinder rang him and told him he couldn't find his wife and kids. To which the answer was – ring her friends and phone back at eight p.m. if he had no joy...' He paused. 'Well, you can see the progression, can't you...? In the event they didn't find their bodies until the next morning. By which time they'd been battered to buggery on the rocks.'

I felt myself shivering. Roberts spoke with a passion and, although it was good to have him on the team, his doubts had held no sway in the past. All this mulling over what had happened still wasn't evidence. Nothing seemed concrete and real. It was all supposition.

Hubert glanced at his watch. If we were

going to have another look round Tamberlake it was time to go.

Roberts noticed. 'If you're going to the
Warrinder place I'll come with you.'

'Dad – don't get involved,' said Liam,
sounding worried. 'Your blood pressure
went up last time. Leave it to Kate.'

'She's an amateur. We're professionals. You
come as well.'

Liam glanced enquiringly at me. I nodded.
I was pleased.

Robert was setting the burglar alarm as we
left the bungalow. He turned to me. 'There
was insurance money,' he said.

'They wouldn't pay out on suicide though
... would they?'

'Not for suicide, but for murder. They were
all insured. His life, two hundred thousand,
her life, a hundred thousand, and the kids,
fifty thousand pounds each. Makes you
think, doesn't it?'

It certainly did.

Fourteen

I knew little about life insurance but again suspicion was not enough. We were following Roberts senior and son. I regretted not telling them I'd seen Paul the night before, just in case Paul was at the house.

In the event all seemed quiet. The sun shone and there was a gentle breeze and Tamberlake looked fairly tranquil. Gill had managed to leave the back door open, although I did see Robert with a huge bunch of keys and I wondered if he could pick locks as well as make keys.

Once inside, Hubert and Roberts went off together. Liam looked enquiringly at me and asked, 'Well where do you want to start?'

'I'm not even sure what we're meant to be looking for.'

'My dad is looking for a body. He's nosed around here before. He had to leave the force on health grounds because of this case. He was forced out. They found out his blood pressure was a bit high and after that he didn't have much choice but to go. He was a thorn in the superintendent's scrotum.'

I could tell Liam shared some of his father's choice turns of phrase but it didn't help me to know exactly what I was meant to be looking for. 'How would you dispose of a body in and around this house?' I asked.

He looked thoughtful and stared at the kitchen table. 'Chopping it up is as good a way as any – if you can face it. That way you can leave the pieces in different locations. But believe me, Kate, there are many people murdered whose bodies are never found. Their graves exist somewhere, but hiding places are so many and varied, including the sea. Well-weighted bodies can stay on the seabed for ever.'

'There is one way he could have got rid of some of the body parts,' I said. 'It's a bit far-fetched but still feasible.'

'Fire away.'

'What about well wrapped up and carried in luggage to Argentina?'

All credit to Liam the gorgeous hunk, he didn't laugh. 'An arm or a chopped-up leg would be easy enough to carry but would the X-ray machines pick it up? Even if the airport staff thought it was a joint of meat, I don't think it's legal to carry fresh meat in passenger luggage.'

'No, I suppose not,' I agreed. Even so, I hadn't given up on the idea entirely. 'What about in the boot of a car? Across the channel by ferry and for a start there's the whole

162

of France to dump the body parts.'

He nodded. 'It's been done before.'

Strange, I thought, here was a man I fancied like mad and, far from flirting with him, we were discussing the disposal of body parts.

'Dad's convinced Alison's body is here somewhere,' he said. 'He even asked for bits of the premises to be dug up.'

'Which bits?'

'Parts of the garden where new plants and bushes had been put in. The gardener was interviewed but Warrinder had been abroad at the time of planting, so a dig was vetoed.'

I was about to tell him that I'd seen Paul locally when he was supposedly still in Argentina. He was a man who always purported to be away at crucial times and yet Fran had died with him in the house. Any further discussion was cut short when Hubert and Roberts appeared.

Roberts looked flushed and angry. 'I'm going to nail the bastard if it's the last thing I do. His passport's gone. He's in some racket up to his neck. I don't know if it's drugs or money-laundering. I think he's leading a double life and travelling on a false passport ... I'm telling you, Liam, I won't rest...'

'Yes, Dad, you will rest and it'll be the long one. Is he worth dying for?'

Roberts took a deep breath. 'I know I get

163

agitated but I was in the force all my life and when you see these well educated prats more concerned about figures and budgets than catching criminals it just makes my blood boil.'

To defuse the situation I said, 'Let's get out of here. It's not giving us any answers.' Then I added, 'Has Hubert told you Warrinder is already in the area? He wasn't due until tomorrow.'

'Where is he? And why didn't you tell me?' snapped Roberts.

'Hang on, Dad,' said Liam, looking daggers at me. 'I didn't know anything about this.'

'I want to know where he is ... now! Don't worry, I'm not planning to take him apart limb from limb. But I'd like to see what he gets up to.'

Liam looked at me and I could see he wasn't best pleased. I shrugged and looked apologetic but it was too late now to stop Roberts. 'He's at Great Marrington,' I said. 'Last house of the village.'

'East or west side?'

'East, I think.'

He raised his eyebrows as if my being unsure of direction was a further indication that I was brainless. The three men went into a brief huddle to exclude me, I suppose, and I stood like a lemon for a few minutes.

By now I was feeling uncomfortable anyway at the four of us trespassing and wanted to get away. Also time was pressing, Hubert was only able to stay for a week and we only had the one car. I could of course hire a car and stay on alone. I had to admit, but only to myself, that I felt overwhelmed. The police had closed the case. Fran and her children had been cremated and although Alison was technically a missing person, she was just one of thousands of the missing not sending Christmas cards. Roberts hadn't managed to make headway whilst he was in the force and now the passage of time had blunted any leads. It was also more than likely that those who had lied at the time would continue to lie.

We went our separate ways but not before I'd given Liam my mobile phone number. 'If you think of anything,' I said casually.

'I'll be in touch,' he said as he briefly clasped my hand.

In the car I asked Hubert why I'd been excluded from their conversation.

'No sinister intent. We've been invited to lunch at their place tomorrow.'

'We haven't got time for that,' I said irritably.

'A working lunch. We need them both on our side. Liam can get us information. Anyway, since when has lunch been such a hardship for you?'

I didn't of course have an answer to that

and it would mean seeing Liam again. So I smiled. 'Where to now then?' I asked.

'I fancy a pint.'

'That means I have to do the driving.'

'My turn today. You can drink tomorrow.'

Hubert drove to Trevelly and into the spacious car park of the Crown and Anchor.

'We need to keep local so that we can catch any gossip,' he said as he locked the car. I looked around the car park; ours was the only car. He noticed my scathing glance. 'It's early yet. It could be crowded inside.'

It wasn't. Inside, there were far more horse brasses than customers. Three old men sat playing dominoes in a dim corner and the young barman was busy doing the *Sun* crossword. It didn't augur well on the gossip front. The barman looked up as we walked to the bar.

'What can I get you, my beauties?' he asked. He had a pale, round face, hazel eyes and fair-cropped hair, and he'd taken lessons in 'camp'.

'I'll have a pint of the local bitter,' said Hubert, his voice seeming lower than usual.

'Good choice, sir, if I may say so. And for the young lady?'

'I'll have an orange juice.'

As he poured the beer he seemed eager to talk. 'Down here on holiday are we, sir? Taking in the lovely Cornish sights?'

Hubert shook his head. 'Not exactly. I've

166

come seeking information about my niece, Alison Peters. She went missing from around these parts.'

I was impressed with Hubert's quick thinking, because I was pretty sure he'd only thought of that on the spur of the moment. The barman was by now opening my bottle of orange juice. 'She was living up at Tamberlake, wasn't she?' he asked, although he obviously knew that she had been. Hubert nodded.

'I've only worked here a year but people still talk about her and the woman who jumped off the cliff with her kids. I reckon the house is jinxed. Some old places are like that.'

He handed me my juice and then Hubert surprised me. 'You go and find a table, Kate. I'll be with you in a minute.'

Find a table! I thought. There was nothing *but* empty tables. But I did as I was told and found a table near a book-lined wall. It was one of those themed pubs which is a cross between a library and an auction room. Hubert seemed to be talking very quietly to the barman and I was intrigued. What the hell was he asking him that he should exclude me? They were talking together for several minutes and I began to get just a little irritated. I'd finished my orange juice by the time Hubert returned. 'Contain yourself,' he said before I could open my mouth. 'I'll explain all.'

Even then Hubert sipped at his beer thoughtfully and I grew more impatient.

'Come on then, spill the beans. What on earth did you find to talk about with the barman?'

'Drugs.'

'Drugs,' I repeated likc a parrot.

'Yes. Robert is convinced Warrinder is involved in drug dealing. It's a belief that marred his career, because he managed to persuade the superintendent of the day that Tamberlake was Cornwall's main storehouse for hard drugs. Paul and Fran were married by then, Fran was pregnant and at six a.m. one morning a "crack" team ... my little joke ... battered down the door dressed all in black and heavily armed. They found nothing. Not even any wacky baccy. The chief constable apologized and Roberts is convinced there was some sort of compensation payout for Warrinder. It seems the Warrinders have lived in Cornwall for generations and had used their money for many good causes. It was embarrassment and recriminations all round.' He paused to take breath.

'You didn't find *any* of that out from the barman, did you?'

'Be patient, Kate. The superintendent of the time was transferred, he took all the blame but of course it had been Roberts who had instigated the whole thing. Any promotion he may have hoped for was scuppered and when he still carried on making waves – they encouraged him to go.' He paused to sip his drink. 'I'll put you out of your misery. I asked the barman who his supplier was.'

My ears caught the words but I was having trouble actually believing it. 'Whatever made you think he'd have one – just because he's gay and camp?'

'Nothing to do with that. His skin had a pasty look and I thought the pupils of his eyes seemed abnormal.'

'I'm very impressed,' I said. Actually I felt peeved that I hadn't noticed but I supposed that was because I'd been distracted by his voice. 'I'd be even more impressed,' I added, 'if he'd told you.'

Hubert grinned. 'He did. I told him I'd got chronic pain and he said he could tell I wasn't a cop. I don't know how he knew that, but he told me there was a wine bar in Newquay – the Marigold. There I was to ask for a man called Big Charlie and if I said Gay Gordon sent me he'd give me what I wanted.'

Suddenly I was worried. Neither of us knew anything about the drugs scene. I read the papers and heard of schoolchildren using and selling drugs, but no one had ever offered me any and in Longborough I wasn't aware of any scene. 'You're getting out of your depth,' I said. 'Silly nicknames are always a bad omen.'

'I haven't done anything yet. Anyway, I'll only be meeting a supplier. It's the dealers we want and, according to Roberts, Warrinder could be big time.'

I sighed. 'I'm getting dodgy vibes about all this.'

'I'll get you another orange juice,' said Hubert, patting my arm, 'and something with chips that'll chase them away.'

I watched Hubert's retreating back and thought, *A portion of chips won't do it this time.* We were merely amateurs and to me illegal drugs spelt only violence and death. There only had to be a whisper that we were not genuine tourists and we could be in trouble. After all, this patch of Cornwall was only small and the Cornish were known for their smuggling abilities. All that differed was the merchandise.

When Hubert came back I asked him when he was meeting Big Charlie.

'Tonight,' he said. 'What's wrong with tonight?'

'Nothing, but I'm coming with you.'

'Oh no you're not.'

'Oh yes I am.' Then I added feebly, 'It is my case after all. You have bodies to attend to in Longborough.'

'You're being silly. People buy drugs every day. It's not dangerous as long as we don't

170

take them.'

I stared at him long and hard. 'Honestly, sometimes I despair, for a man of your age you can be very naïve.'

Hubert merely grinned. 'Look on it as an adventure, Kate.'

'I think,' I said miserably, 'it's one adventure we could do without.'

Fifteen

During lunch I realized Hubert was determined to follow the drugs line of enquiry, although how he expected buying a few quid's worth of crack cocaine would aid our investigation I didn't know. All he did was murmur about 'little acorns' and refuse to say any more.

We did agree our next priority was to try to talk to as many friends and associates of Paul as possible. I had a feeling that Paul had kept *his* friends close and Alison and Fran's at bay. Hubert produced a map of Trevelly and the surrounding area and found out that two people on our list of six 'regulars' lived near enough to walk to Tamberlake approximately two miles away. We'd already seen Jamie, so it left a mere five to go. Which didn't sound like many on paper but the reality always works out to be more difficult.

We walked Jasper for a short distance but he seemed glad enough to snuggle down on the back seat. We left the back window open just in case we forgot about him. The weather remained warm and mellow but sun through glass can heat a car to suffocating levels, so we were both conscious of Jasper's welfare.

Our first call was to Michelle Ford. The terraced house, modest but attractive, with hanging baskets on the porch and rose bushes in the front garden, was situated on the outskirts of Trevelly. Hubert parked the car directly outside. 'What's our cover story?' he asked.

'Journalists?' I suggested. 'We're done with the police angle.'

He shook his head. 'No, it's too easy to say no to journalists.'

I thought for a moment. Jamie would undoubtedly have told them the police were snooping around and our descriptions would have been circulated. 'What about saying we're really insurance investigators trying to establish if Alison is dead or alive? After seven years of being missing with no contact, someone can be pronounced dead – can't they?'

Hubert nodded but still looked uncertain. 'I think it's time to come clean. Just say you're a PI and leave it at that. If they won't talk to us we'll have to think of something else.'

In the event it didn't matter, there was no reply to our loud knocking. So loud that an elderly toothless neighbour came out and said in a crackly voice, 'It's no use knocking.

She doesn't get home till late.'

'How late is late?' I asked.

'Between seven and half past. Shall I tell her who called?'

'No thanks, we'll come back.'

'Right you are.'

A bit dejected we drove on to the next address. The home of Harvey Trenchard. A modern detached house this time, low-level, with vast picture windows and what looked like solar panelling on the roof. It reminded me of a goldfish bowl and although the house was well back from the road, almost hidden by an array of trees, as we drove through the open gates it wasn't long before we glimpsed a man at the window watching our arrival.

He came to the door, a short round man, in his early forties, wearing gold-rimmed glasses that reminded me of an agitated owl. I decided Hubert was right. 'Kate Kinsella,' I said, 'private investigator, and my associate Hubert Humberstone.'

'I don't want to talk to you,' he snapped. 'I've lost two good friends in recent years and I don't want to rake up the past.'

It was obvious if I didn't say the right thing now he was going to slam the door in our faces, so I took a deep breath. 'Helen Woods is a long-standing friend of mine. She wants to marry Paul, of course she does, but she thinks the house is haunted and I wondered

174

if you'd ever noticed anything unusual at Tamberlake.'

Harvey moved his glasses further down his nose and stared at me above the rims. His eyes were cold brown pebbles. 'When a house has seen tragedy, it's bound to leave its mark,' he said. 'But I've never experienced anything untoward there. The best person to talk to is the estate agent who has tried to sell the house on at least two occasions.'

'Fine. Thank you,' I replied. 'The name of the agents?'

'Brant and Brant. Trevelly High Street.' With that terse reply he did indeed slam the door.

'Pompous prat!' I proclaimed as we turned to go.

'Calm down,' said Hubert. 'One of the group will talk to us.'

'I don't think so,' I said despondently. 'They lied en masse about being at Tamberlake on the night Fran died. I can't see them recanting now.'

We walked back to the car in silence. I turned once to see the 'owl' watching us from his glass bowl. I found him quite sinister and wondered how he afforded a house of that size. 'What do you think he does for a living?' I asked.

Hubert smiled at me and patted me on the head. 'No use guessing. Roberts will know and if he doesn't, Liam will find out for us.'

I brightened at the sound of Liam's name and the fact that I'd be seeing him for lunch the next day.

It took only a few minutes to find Brant and Brant but it was a surprisingly busy office with a team of three sitting in front of computers and each having a potential customer in front of them. The young receptionist wore a short skirt, a flimsy white blouse, high heels and a switch-on smile. I told her we were interested in buying Tamberlake and with a big apologetic smile she told me it wasn't on the market but there were other large houses which she was sure I'd love. We took a seat and she handed us details of four houses which she was sure would fit our 'requirements'. I flicked through the brochures, for they were brochures and not flimsy two-pagers.

'I reckon,' I whispered to Hubert, 'she's seen your car and thinks you're my sugar daddy.'

'Hmm. If I were,' he said thoughtfully, 'I'd want you to look like a rich bitch. Dripping gold and diamonds, with blood-red three-inch fingernails and six-inch heels.'

'Pigs might fly,' I said as my eyes glazed over at the most expensive of the houses – a cool £3,000,000. 'And they'd be flying if, between us, we could afford the porch and the conservatory in these houses.'

'You have no ambition, Kate, that's your

trouble.'

Since he hadn't bothered to look at the prices I didn't respond and a few minutes later one of the prospective buyers was being guided to the door and having his hand firmly shaken. The redundant negotiator now turned his attention to us. In his early thirties, short and dapper, he wore a navy suit and white shirt. His hair was thick and dark and had a crimpiness that was probably natural but looked artificial. He struck me as the type who would wear sunglasses on the dullest day. 'Hi, I'm Simon Viner,' he announced with a wide smile, thrusting his hand at us and shaking our hands vigorously. He guided us to his desk, lifting out the chair for me, but his attitude changed immediately we mentioned Tamberlake. 'You do know it's not up for sale?'

'Oh yes,' I said innocently. 'But we've heard a whisper that the owner, Paul Warrinder, is planning to marry and he's thinking about selling again.'

Simon's small mouth curved a little. 'Well, I hope he gives us another crack at selling it.'

'You've had problems with it?' queried Hubert.

'No, not at all. In fact an American wanted to buy it, convinced it was really "Mandalay".' Noticing Hubert's puzzled expression he added, 'From the novel by Daphne du Maurier.'

'Oh yes. I remember,' said Hubert. 'I saw the film.'

'When was it you tried to sell it?' I asked Simon.

'The first time Mr Warrinder put it on the market was about five years back. I'd just started work here. I was too junior to deal with it then. But when his wife was alive, we did have one or two interested besides the American.'

'Why didn't it sell then?'

Simon shook his head. 'I got the impression that Mr Warrinder didn't really *want* to sell. It was an inflated price and he refused to drop.'

'Do you think that was because he was emotionally involved with the house?' I asked. Simon's answering glance made it obvious he'd never given that a thought.

'Could be. The Warrinders have lived there since Victorian times. Old man Warrinder – didn't marry until he was fifty – and young Warrinder's mother died in a car crash. The story is the family money had all been given away to good Cornish causes and there was only the house left to the only son and heir. These big houses do take considerable maintenance...' He paused as if remembering he was a salesman. 'Now, I can show you more modern houses, easy to maintain, some with solar panels.'

'I saw one of those yesterday. I thought it

was like a goldfish bowl.'

'I'm surprised. Our new boss, Mr Trenchard, designed his own.'

Time for a hasty exit, I thought, but I kept my cool. 'I would have thought Brant would have been the owner.'

'Mr Brant and his daughter have just sold up and moved abroad. We'll be called Trenchard soon.'

I smiled at him. 'I'm sure it'll be Trenchard and Viner before very long. Thank you so much for your help. We'll be in touch.'

His face grew slightly pink and his final handshake at the door was even more energetic.

'Phew!' I breathed as we walked away. 'Why the hell did Trenchard send us there?'

'A wild goose chase?' suggested Hubert.

'Or just trying to wear us out. At this rate Helen will be celebrating her first anniversary before we come up with anything concrete on Paul.'

Again we checked our list, deciding to make it our last house call of the day. Our other visit was to be the druggie wine bar in the evening. The name of the second female on the Saturday night list was Diane Brandon. Her apartment in a large Edwardian house was in a quiet avenue of trees on the approach road to Trevelly. There were no nets at the window and an intercom system. There seemed to be no sign of life. I pressed the first of the other two buttons and there was still no response. The top-flat occupant did respond. 'I'm looking for Diane,' I said into the microphone panel.

'She's on holiday. Won't be back till the weekend,' came the voice from above.

'Cheers.'

I felt despondent as I got back in the car. All we'd managed was to receive the order of the elbow from one friend and by now they would all be forewarned and forearmed. Why would they change their stories now? To admit they met up as usual on the Saturday night that Fran killed herself would be pointless unless they had a reason to tell the truth.

Hubert, sensing I was losing heart, said, 'Come on, we'll have a few pre-dinner drinkies at the hotel and take a taxi tonight.'

'It's only five,' I said.

'By the time we've given Jasper a walk and fed him it'll easily be six and then we need to freshen up – it won't leave that much drinking time.'

Nothing ever goes quite according to plan and as we walked through the lounge a voice called out, 'Kate!'

I turned to see Gill coming towards us. 'Why didn't you phone me?' I asked.

'I did,' she said indignantly. 'You were switched off.'

Hubert, not waiting to be introduced,

slunk away to walk Jasper. Gill looked a little flushed and worried. I ordered a pot of tea and we sat alone in a corner of the lounge by the potted plants. 'I'm going tonight,' she said. 'I've had a huge row with Helen. She's found out you're back and making enquiries. In the end I told her I was paying you to investigate Paul. She went ballistic. She was a different person. Shouting that we were both jealous bitches who couldn't find a decent man of our own. And Paul was practically the Son of God and how dare we suggest he'd done anything criminal?'

'So what do we do now?' I asked.

Gill shook her head. 'I wish I'd never got involved. The way I feel at the moment I won't be coming to the wedding.'

'Has anything else happened? Does she know he's in Cornwall at the moment?'

Gill grimaced. 'No ... she doesn't. I don't think she'd have believed me anyway.'

Our tray of tea arrived delivered by a heavy-footed waitress with a sour expression. I poured the tea and handed a cup to Gill. 'She's not as innocent in all this as she appears, you know. That photo of her sitting on the wall behind Fran and the children wasn't a coincidence. She'd been seeing him for a few weeks before Fran died.'

'She admitted that?'

'Not exactly. She said it was merely an innocent friendship and that they'd only met

181

for coffee or afternoon tea.'

'Maybe that's the truth,' I said.

'Well one thing was true,' she agreed. 'They had met in a camera shop. But everyone in Cornwall knows of Paul Warrinder. It's a small place and old man Warrinder funded amongst other things two libraries and a park. They were always in the local newspaper. There was a full-page spread for his wedding to Fran.'

'So, she knew of him long before he met Fran?'

Gill nodded. 'It's no wonder the poor cow topped herself and the children. She must have found out for sure that day. Maybe someone let the cat out of the bag that night at the dinner party. She goes to bed, the bastard lying fast asleep beside her, and she decides that she and the kids would be better off in the next world.'

I had to agree Gill had probably got it right. Their so-called friends must have felt guilty and so declined to admit they were even there that night. There may of course have been a massive row and perhaps they had left earlier than usual.

'And there's another thing,' she said, as she added another spoonful of sugar to her tea. 'I searched his pockets and found a card from a gambling casino – Knightsbridge – pretty exclusive by the looks of it.'

From her pocket she produced the card.

Gold-embossed and gold by name – 'The Golden Globe'.

It seemed to me that, far from going abroad, Paul was spending regular amounts of time in London. But were the gym and a casino the only reasons?

'How did you leave it with Helen?'

'Frosty to say the least. I don't think she'll be wanting either of us at the wedding.'

We sat silently for a while. 'I think we should call the whole thing off,' said Gill eventually. 'She isn't the friend I thought she was and if she makes a mistake that's her lookout.'

I felt inclined to agree with her and was about to say, *Yes, let's forget it*, when I remembered Roberts and his suspicions. Suspicions that bordered on obsession, but he was an experienced detective and I couldn't ignore that.

'You go back to London, Gill. Hubert and I have got contacts now. I can't let it go. It's not really about Helen, is it? It's about the two other women involved with Paul who both came to sticky ends.'

'You think Alison is dead?'

'Yes. I do. And I think Paul murdered her. But how the hell we can prove it I don't know.'

'Wow, what a mess,' she sighed. 'But ... there is something I could do. I could check out the gym and the casino for you. Even if I only found out the membership fees and where he stayed in London.'

'That's a good idea.'

Gill glanced at her watch. 'I must go. It'll be really late when I get back.'

I walked with her to the car and I watched her drive away until she was just a little flash of red in the distance. An image that reminded me of the red of the collapsed strawberry gateau. A cold shiver snaked down my back and I didn't know why.

Sixteen

We arrived in the dining room a little late, to find our usual table for two in the corner was gone, usurped by a man with two walking sticks, so it would have been churlish to object. We were shown instead to a table for four and I prayed no one would be sat with us. Eating with strangers can be hell. How people manage it on cruises I'll never know. Of course, everyone is a stranger at first but there are some people who should definitely remain in that category.

During the first course, which was called 'seafood surprise' as opposed to prawn cocktail, I told Hubert about Gill's visit and that I felt uneasy. He told me I was worrying too much. 'Next step is you starting to believe Tamberlake really is haunted. It's best if we concentrate on the drugs angle at the moment.'

'We don't even know if there is a drugs angle.'

'True,' he agreed, 'but we still need to eliminate it.'

'I've done nothing about those watercolours either. I'd like to know if they are as good as I think they are. After all, why would Paul alter Fran's signature on them if it wasn't worth his while?'

'Who knows? Does he have any talents of his own? He may have been jealous.'

If that was Hubert's psychological angle I wasn't convinced, but I supposed it was a possibility.

'There was that photo of him on a horse playing polo,' I said. 'Supposedly in Argentina. Probably a mock-up taken in some local park.'

'Don't get impatient,' said Hubert. 'This is complicated. It could take weeks, even months. Look at poor Robert Roberts – he's been pursuing Warrinder for years and he hasn't made much progress.'

'That's really cheered me up.'

'Think of it this way. Roberts has got us on his side now.' I wasn't convinced that was really to his advantage but I didn't say so.

Our main course had just been served when we were interrupted by the late arrival at our table of two large middle-aged Americans both wearing shorts. My heart sank. After introductions and handshakes Hubert announced he was a funeral director. I thought that might have caused a real hiatus in the 'getting-to-know-you stakes', instead Franklin and Beatrice didn't bat an eyelid, because they were aficionados of English graveyards.

Luckily Beatrice wasn't as talkative as Franklin and I could have learnt more about epitaphs and who was buried where, than most people get to know in a lifetime. But I was only half listening. I couldn't concentrate on official graves when I was concerned with the unofficial, unknown grave of a young woman.

After our dessert Hubert and I made an apologetic escape with Franklin's raucous 'We'll be seeing you folks!' ringing in our ears.

In the taxi, which thankfully had turned up on time, Hubert made it plain I was to sit still and keep my mouth shut. 'Are you actually going to part with good money?' I asked. He nodded. 'Don't worry, I'll buy the gear, then hand it over to young Roberts tomorrow and he can deal with it.' I still wasn't happy about Hubert taking such a chance, but he still sounded cautious so I tried to relax and enjoy the drive.

It had crossed my mind that Hubert might have been planning to sample the goods. After all, he didn't smoke and he rarely took as much as an aspirin, so I thought he might be tempted by curiosity and a misplaced sense of adventure. But now I realized he was far too sensible – he just wanted to meet a supplier – all in the cause of our investigation.

It was just after nine when the taxi driver dropped us off just outside the Star Light Wine Bar. He promised to pick us up just before midnight. It was dark outside and nearly as dark inside. The bar was obviously named after its interior, because the ceiling held myriad star-shaped lights and the chairs and tables were the brightest chrome. But the light remained so subdued that the few customers milling around seemed to be moving in the shadows. I found a table near a wall and watched as Hubert approached the bar. He came back in high dudgeon claiming, 'Daylight bloody robbery! Two glasses of cheap plonk and it cost more than a whole bottle of a good supermarket wine.'

'That's life,' I said. 'Just wait until you find out how much your little packet of crack will cost.'

'I've heard it's not that expensive.'

'Not at first maybe. But an addict is in no position to haggle once hooked. They have to pay the going price.'

'Just sip that wine slowly, Kate. You can buy the next round.'

'It's no wonder you're a rich man.'

Hubert scowled and his face appeared to be strangely mottled in the 'star' light.

We sat in silence watching a few more customers arrive. Mostly young men, smartly casual. A sign on the door had announced 'No jeans or trainers'. There was some hugging and shaking hands, except that soon it became obvious that the hands were still being held and that the hugs became a lover's possessive clasp. It took Hubert a little time to realize what was going on. 'This is a gay men's club,' he said in astonishment.

'Well at least *I* won't be bothered,' I said smugly.

'What's that supposed to mean?' asked Hubert, his eyes roving over the increasing huddles.

'You could well be a source of ... interest.'

He couldn't see that I was merely winding him up and he turned to gaze at me with an anxious expression. 'They'll see I'm straight.'

'It's not stamped on your forehead.'

He didn't say another word for a while, then, as if he'd been mulling the issue over, he muttered, 'If someone did ... proposition me ... what do I say?'

'I'd suggest "get lost" but if you want to be more subtle just say you're not alone.'

'Will that work?'

'Probably not, if they like a challenge.'

'You're being a real pain.'

My comeuppance came about fifteen minutes later when a group of women arrived together, some of whom looked very butch. One with short-cropped hair and vast shoulders kept looking my way. I wasn't nervous, just a little disconcerted, but an hour and one more drink later we began to relax. Nothing riotous was going on, in fact the atmosphere felt safe and friendly. Apart from a few casual glances, no one bothered us.

'There you are,' I said to Hubert. 'In the gay world we are not fanciable.'

'I'm not fancied in any world,' replied Hubert, gloomily staring into his wine glass.

It was nearly eleven when Hubert spotted his quarry. 'That's him,' he whispered in my ear. My eyes scanned the little groups around the bar. 'Don't make it obvious,' he urged. 'He might get suspicious.'

I didn't see why he should but I could tell Hubert was quite excited by the whole thing. 'Which one?' I whispered back.

'The big bloke over by the corner of the bar – that's Big Charlie.'

I looked across to the bar as casually as I could. Big Charlie had his back to me and was talking to the barman. He was well over six feet tall with broad shoulders, a square head, and was all dressed in black. 'He looks like a cop to me,' I said. 'Do be careful.'

Hubert finished his drink. 'Just stay here,' he said. 'It won't take long.' He walked over to the bar and, as the barman began serving another customer, Hubert stood alongside Big Charlie and engaged him in conversation. It wasn't long before Hubert and Big Charlie strolled off towards the gents', Big Charlie first, followed a few seconds later by Hubert.

I debated for a while about buying myself another glass of wine. Neither of us was driving, so I approached the bar, having to negotiate a small group of women. They smiled at me as I eased past them and the big butch one said, in a surprisingly soft voice, 'If you're on your own you can always stand with us. I'm Denise, known as Den.' So I bought my drink and stood listening to their chat, which centred mostly on their jobs, clothes, food and diets and holidays. I was enjoying myself just listening when a crop-haired blonde with a face like a cherub asked me what I did for a living. I'd blurted out the truth before thinking. 'Hey, that's cool. How did you get into that? Come on, tell us all about it.'

Much to my shame I forgot about time and Hubert. I was enjoying myself, they were a lively crowd and they seemed interested in my job. In a lull in the conversation I glanced at my watch. I'd been chatting for half an hour! Where the hell was Hubert? The look on my face alerted Den. 'What's up?'

'I'll have to go. My ... colleague ... he should have been back by now.'

'Where did he go?'

'The gents'.'

I'd already moved away when she grabbed my arm. 'I'll come with you.'

She strode ahead with me following. At the

door of the gents' she held up her hand. 'I'll go in first. No one will argue with me – tallish balding guy, isn't he?' I nodded.

I heard her open the cubicle doors and a flustered-looking man came rushing out. When she reappeared it was simply to shake her head and ask, 'Was he alone?'

'No, he was with Big Charlie.'

'Shit!'

'You know him?'

'Everyone knows him. He's a thug. What in God's name did he want with him?'

'He was trying to buy crack cocaine. It was a lead in our investigation.'

'A bloody dangerous lead.'

I could feel the panic rising in me now. My chest felt tight, my mouth dry.

'There's a back entrance,' said Den. 'Come on.'

We rushed past the ladies' and a staff room to the door at the end of the corridor. As Den opened it a security light came on, showing a small walled area with overflowing bins. There was no sign of Hubert. 'I'll check outside the gate,' said Den. She heaved the tall wooden gate open and looked around outside. I meanwhile had spotted something on the ground near the bins. Even with the security lights on it looked like oil. I bent down and rubbed my finger in it and stroked it on to my hand. It was blood. I couldn't move and I began to heave. Den helped me to my feet. 'Now, don't panic. You'd better call the police.'

'And say what? A friend of mine went off with Big Charlie to the gents' loo to buy crack cocaine. I don't think they'd have much sympathy.'

I'd begun to shiver now. I had a feeling I wasn't going to see Hubert ever again. I couldn't think and I allowed Den to guide me back to the bar. As we ended, a bell for time was being rung. 'Your best bet,' said Den, 'is to go back to where you're staying and ring the local hospital.'

'I've got a taxi booked for midnight,' I murmured.

'Right, I'll come with you.' She propped me up by the bar, where her friends had gathered round wanting to know what was going on. Someone thrust my handbag towards me and then Den, with her hand under my elbow, guided me outside to the car park. The taxi was driving in at the same time and we bundled in and he drove off. Even though I tried to keep calm, tears pricked at my eyelids and I couldn't think. I had no idea what to do next.

'Have you got any friends in the area?' asked Den.

'Friends,' I echoed. Then like a ray of sunlight through fog came my answer. 'I know an ex-cop.'

'Ring him, ring him now.'

I scrabbled about in my bag and finally found Roberts's business card. I punched out the wrong number twice until Den grabbed my mobile and the card and did it for me. Roberts sounded wide awake. I gave him a garbled account. 'Don't worry, Kate. Go back to the hotel and stay there. Lock your door and don't answer it to anyone. I'll get Liam and his mates out looking for Big Charlie's car. We know the number. Don't you worry, we won't pussyfoot when we do find him.' Never mind Big Charlie, I thought, what about Hubert?

The bar was closed at the Regis but Den had a word with the night porter and he appeared minutes later with a bottle of brandy. 'Sorry about your trouble,' he said. 'Make sure you give me a replacement tomorrow.'

Luckily Hubert had left his room key in reception, because I'd forgotten all about Jasper. As I approached Hubert's room Jasper began to bark. When I opened the door with Den still in attendance he seemed more interested in Den than me. She was obviously a dog lover and next door in my room, whilst she made a fuss of Jasper, I poured two large brandies into teacups. I was still shivery and on the verge of tears but the brandy's fiery warmth braced me a little. It was odd, I thought, that I should be relying on a woman I'd only just met, but it was her calm masculine style that was so reassuring. I supposed we could scour the country for Hubert but where would we start? If the police did find Big Charlie he would probably admit to supplying drugs but not to ... what? Abduction? GBH? Murder? I downed another brandy. 'Hubert's dead,' I said aloud.

'You can't know that,' said Den. 'You're going to have to get a grip.'

I knew she was right but I couldn't. I had visions of Hubert crawling away to die. In pain, lonely.

'I've got to go and look for him,' I said. 'I can't stay here.'

'Didn't that ex-cop say to stay here with the door locked?'

'Yeah. But I've got to *do* something.'

'Let's wait for an hour or so and see what happens.'

Her quiet voice calmed me for a few seconds. Then the thought galloped into my mind that in an hour or so Hubert could have bled to death. Judging by the amount of blood in the yard he could have bled to death in minutes. Please, Hubert, I pleaded silently. Please still be alive.

Seventeen

Den did her best to make me talk about something other than Hubert and although I tried to respond I could only do so pacing the room. She was, it seems, a fire officer and at any other time I would have been really interested – but not now. Images of Hubert lying dead by some roadside kept coming to mind. Jasper's interest in Den had now waned and for a while he followed me as I walked back and forth. Then after a few minutes he sat at the door to the garden wagging his tail and barking. I opened the door and he rushed off into the dark.

I was so consumed with worrying about Hubert I didn't notice how long Jasper had been gone. 'There's no sign of Jasper,' said Den, peering out into the garden. 'I can't see him.' I stood at the door and called him but he didn't come running. The garden was walled, with the gate as the only exit. After that a short path led to the car park. There was no way he could escape – unless the gate had been left open. It was then that Jasper gave a short sharp yap.

I rushed out into the garden and found Jasper frantically trying to burrow beneath the gate. I opened it and he immediately tore off towards the car park. As we ran after him the security lights came on. There were at least twenty parked cars and we lost sight of Jasper amongst them. Den and I stood calling him and finally he responded with excited yapping. The sound was coming from beyond the furthest car, somewhere in the bushes and the flowerbeds. And there lying face down was Hubert. I knew it was him because I recognized his new casual shoes. His hands were outstretched and he was clutching a syringe, the needle shining in the semi-black. It was Den who took charge, rolling him on his side, checking his airway. 'He's still alive,' she said. From her trouser pocket she produced a mobile phone. She rang 999 while I stayed on my knees looking in horror at Hubert's face. His lower lip was bloody and swollen, his eyes puffed and closed. There was blood covering his face and the rivulets had dried into his neck. He was breathing but only just. I rolled up his sleeves to see if he'd been pumped full of heroin but in the poor light I couldn't see the needle puncture.

I held his hand and began talking to him. 'Come on, Hubert. Hang on. You're going to be all right.' All the usual stuff. I wasn't convinced he could hear me but it was worth a try. Den rushed off to get a blanket and I changed tack. 'Don't you dare leave me,' I said directly into his ear. 'I can't carry on without you.' He made a slight gurgling sound and I thought at first he was trying to respond but he was only attempting to spit out a loose tooth. I pushed the tooth back into the socket and then Den came rushing back with the blanket. I'd just covered him when I heard the ambulance siren. No sound ever could have been more welcome.

The paramedics were quick and efficient. An oxygen mask was strapped to Hubert's face, an intravenous line was put in place but when they asked what exactly had happened to him I couldn't say. 'Is he a druggie?' the younger paramedic asked me as he carefully removed the syringe from Hubert's hand. 'No way,' I said. 'He's a funeral director.' It was a daft answer but I wasn't thinking that well. My knees were beginning to buckle and I had a desperate need for confirmation that he would survive. But my nursing experience told me that though the paramedics would do their best there were no guarantees.

Once he was stabilized I walked behind them, planning to be with him in the ambulance, but I was told I would have to follow on behind. Den came to my rescue again. 'I'll drive you. I only had a sip of the brandy.' Words couldn't express at that moment how grateful I felt towards her. I muttered, 'Thanks a million,' and we quickly made our way to Hubert's car.

We followed close behind the speeding ambulance, with its silent flashing blue light. It all seemed surreal, like watching an accident documentary. But this *was* for real and Hubert's life was on the line and I felt sick.

Mile after mile passed by. 'Where the hell are we going?' I asked Den.

She sped round a tight bend like a rally driver and said, 'We're on the Exeter road.'

'Exeter?' I asked in amazement.

'Yep. Not all the local hospitals have A&E departments. Don't worry, the hospital will know the ambulance is on its way. They'll be all geared up for him.'

The journey seemed to last for an eternity but eventually we arrived and as we parked the car I could see Hubert already being trundled hurriedly into the A&E department.

There was no need for me to run anymore, so we walked slowly and I took deep steadying breaths. Hubert, I knew, would immediately be whisked away into the resuscitation area and there I would be in the way.

The middle-aged male receptionist wore a white tee shirt from which bulged muscular hairy arms. He wanted the usual information: name, address, date of birth, next of kin. I was standing by the desk, feeling distinctly odd and fixated on his hairy arms. I didn't know Hubert's year of birth. His actual birthday was in December but even though I knew the date I couldn't remember it. How could I then say I was his next of kin?

Mr Muscles stared at me and I tried to focus on his name badge. It took me a few seconds – *Norman Jacks*. 'Are you all right?' he asked. My head throbbed, my eyesight seemed dulled and his voice sounded so quiet, as if he were speaking down a long rubber tube. I felt a hand on my shoulder and Den guiding me to a chair and sitting me down with my head between my knees. Thought processes were still in action, though, because I realized that at least it would give me time to do a little mental arithmetic.

When my head resurfaced I was able to tell him 10th December 1948 and my name was Kate Humberstone – daughter. The year was a mere guess but I thought the 10th December was his correct birthday. Norman Jacks filled out the appropriate forms and we joined a sad little band in the waiting area. Every time a door opened our eyes looked towards the person entering for some sign it was us they were looking for.

Waiting in A&E is a lesson in patience but who wants it? Some people just can't cope and a scruffy drunk who had wandered in with a bleeding head wound was one. A security man with a mere half of Norman's muscles attempted to quieten him down. A stream of foul language, mostly unintelligible, followed and when the drunk lashed out at the security guard Den was on her feet and in an instant she had him in an armlock and began wrestling him to the floor. The security man was meanwhile using his walkie-talkie to summon back-up. The drunk by now was lying very still and gingerly Den got to her feet and looked down at him. She looked worried. After all, in the present climate, if she'd injured him, or worse still he was dead, she'd be either sued or imprisoned for five years.

Two more security men burst in then, hauled the drunk to his feet and unceremoniously plonked him into a wheelchair and pushed him away. I wondered where they were taking him but I didn't care and the relief all round that he'd been dispatched was palpable in the air.

Den also looked relieved as she sat down beside me, pink-faced and breathing only a little faster than normal. 'I didn't expect all this on a girls' night out.'

'You were great,' I said admiringly.

'Yeah. Being in the fire service keeps you fit.'

Now that the waiting area was quiet again

we sat silently and in the silence anxiety clawed in the pit of my stomach. Why was it taking so long? When would someone speak to me? I'd already decided that the next medical-looking person to come through the door would be waylaid. For all I knew, Hubert could be in a corridor somewhere. I'd read the newspapers about the elderly lying in corridors for hours, even days. Patience is only a virtue, I decided, when nothing is to be gained by being impatient. If I was playing the 'daughter', then I was going to be a stroppy one and fight for my 'father's' rights.

I stood up and announced to Den, 'I'm going to find out what's going on – now!'

And then, as if conjured from nowhere, a young woman wearing a white coat and a stethoscope strung around her neck like a badge of office walked up to me. 'Are you Kate?' I nodded. She was smiling. 'I'm the registrar, Dr Sophie Morgan. I've just come to tell you you can see your father now. He's going to be fine...' She carried on explaining something about X-rays and cracked ribs but somehow the information wasn't penetrating. *He's going to be fine,* was all that mattered. She led me to a curtained cubicle and, before pulling back the curtain, said, 'I'll need to talk to you again later. Please come and find me before you go. He's still very sleepy due to the heroin.'

I caught the slight note of reproach in her voice but I managed to remain silent. Hubert was going to live and that was all I cared about at the moment.

He lay slightly propped against white pillows. His intravenous infusion continued in his left arm. Both eyes were puffed and blackening and until the swelling went down he would be unable to see. I thought at first he was asleep but then he spoke, 'Will the girls still fancy me now?'

'Did they ever?'

'That's my Kate,' he said. 'I can't see a thing at the moment but I knew it was you.'

'How?'

'Footsteps. You're a bit of a clomper.'

'Shall I go and exchange myself for a ballet dancer?'

'I'm too spaced out for all this, Kate. I keep drifting off. I was set up.'

'Even I guessed that. Was it Big Charlie?'

'Yeah. And two others. One was the barman from the Crown and Anchor. The other was skinny and weasel-faced. I did try to fight back...'

'Don't worry about that. The odds were against you.'

'I've been a bloody fool.'

'We both have. You just need to rest up and get better now. What did they say is wrong with you?'

'Didn't the doctor speak to you?'

'Yes ... but I didn't take it in.'

'Call yourself a nurse?'

'No, at the moment I call myself an anxious relative.'

He grinned through swollen lips, showing one loose front tooth hanging lower than its twin did.

'I wouldn't smile for a while,' I said.

'That tooth,' he said, 'has got to be saved. The doc doesn't hold out much hope. She said I was long in the tooth anyway.'

'A dentist will sort you out.'

'I'm lucky. I've got three broken ribs, bruised kidneys, a half-knocked-out tooth, black eyes and a bloodstream full of heroin, so at the moment I can't feel a thing.'

'When does the doc say you can get out of here?'

'Forty-eight hours if my waterworks function again.'

'Great. I think you ought to go home then, don't you?'

He fumbled for my hand, patted it and said cheerfully, 'Stop talking, Kate. Go home. Go to bed. If I'm lucky some nubile young nurse will give me a blanket bath, so I'm in no rush to go back to Longborough.'

'You'll be lucky. You have to be at death's door to get a blanket bath these days.'

'You're a real killjoy.'

'You wait and see.'

I kissed him on the forehead and was about

to leave when he asked, 'Is Liam with you?'

'No. A woman from the wine bar called Den has been my guardian angel.'

'You mean, she's a...'

'Yes, a lesbian. So what?'

'Well just because you can't find a man doesn't mean you should go the other way.'

'I *could* find a man if I wanted to. And I am *not* going the other way. It's not a matter of choice.'

As Hubert grunted and pretended to snore I made my exit.

Den was still waiting for me in reception. She looked tired now and as I approached she was wearily running her fingers through her hair. I told her about Hubert's condition and that the heroin was keeping him cheerful. We still had the drive back to Trevelly, so I offered her Hubert's room for a few hours' sleep and she agreed. 'I'm not on shift tomorrow,' she said, adding, 'and I'm glad. I feel shattered.' I too felt drained but the awful anxiety had gone.

Den insisted on driving, she was obviously impressed by the car and she was a good, if fast, driver. Her night vision was considerably better than mine.

We'd been driving along for about three miles when my mobile rang. It was Liam. He and his dad had been scouring the countryside for Hubert and Big Charlie and I had forgotten to ring him. I apologized profusely and told him all about Hubert.

'Just as long as you're OK. We haven't found Big Charlie yet but we will, and the others. Make lunch a bit later tomorrow, say two p.m.'

I was surprised lunch was still on. I hadn't given either Helen or Gill or Warrinder a thought. I was at that stage in an investigation when it seems to be going nowhere and where my spirits sink. I'd experienced it before and knew it would pass but there was one thing I simply had to do. I had to confront Paul Warrinder as soon as possible.

Eighteen

The next morning at nine a.m. I rang the hospital. Hubert was both 'satisfactory and comfortable'. I knocked on Hubert's door but Den didn't respond, so I left her to sleep on for a while and rang the hotel manager. He'd heard about Hubert being found unconscious in the car park and was sympathetic and said he'd send up two breakfast trays.

Den was awake by the time breakfast arrived and we ate together in Hubert's room. By the time we'd eaten enough calories to last twenty-four hours I'd told her the whole story. She was a good listener and she told me the drug scene in Newquay was particularly active. 'There's two Cornwalls,' she said as she finished off the last morsel of toast, 'one for the middle-aged and elderly – all cream teas and Cornish pasties – and the other Cornwall for the young – surfing, sex and drugs.'

'So what are the police doing about it?'

She shrugged, pushed her tray to the end of the bed and sat back against the pillows.

'They try, but who's going to give away their supplier?'

'Where does it come from?'

Den's expression revealed she thought I'd led a sheltered life. 'Have you been abroad lately?'

I shook my head. 'I went to New Zealand nearly two years ago.'

'I go to Holland quite often. I've got a good friend there. Back in the UK, customs officials just aren't there to monitor all the flights. I could have walked through any time with a suitcase full of drugs.'

I finished my coffee and took both trays and placed them outside the bedroom door. Drug smuggling, it seemed to me, was too big a leap from possible murder and it complicated everything. If Warrinder was a drug dealer and smuggler and Fran had found out, surely divorce was the answer and not suicide and murder. She could, of course, have shopped him – so why didn't she? Did Alison disappear so completely because, once she found out, she was afraid for her life? Then she must have made a conscious decision to start a new life, not even daring to send her half-brother a Christmas card. In the event that she had evidence of Warrinder being a major drug dealer, surely she would have been offered police protection. That was a question I could save for my lunch with Liam.

Later, when Den was ready to go, I offered her a lift but she declined, saying she'd already booked a minicab. I waited with her in reception and we exchanged telephone numbers, vowing to keep in touch. As we hugged each other goodbye, she murmured in my ear, 'Take care, Kate. There is always someone bent on the inside. It only takes one.' I asked her to explain but the minicab driver was already sounding his horn impatiently and she hurried away.

'Thanks a million,' I shouted after her.

I took time that morning deciding what to wear. In the end I decided on a denim skirt, a tightish black tee shirt and a pair of mules with heels. Checking myself in the mirror I decided Liam would be impressed that I'd scrubbed up so well. Jasper was lying in his basket fast asleep after chasing around the garden. He'd been slightly subdued since finding Hubert and I debated with myself if I should disturb him or not. In the end I chose to leave him behind but asked one of the porters, Jimmy, to let him out for a run mid-afternoon.

I arrived for lunch on the dot of two, which was just as well, because I was quickly ushered into the kitchen and there to greet me was a huge bowl of pasta with a prawn, bacon and cheese sauce. I wasn't a bit hungry but Liam was and he couldn't wait to eat. I was impressed with his cooking but I was more impressed with the fact that he didn't *talk* about the food or his cooking prowess. He asked first about Hubert but I got the impression he wanted to satisfy his stomach and curiosity could wait. So I simply said, 'He's OK – thanks.'

'Come on then, Kate. Eat up. You look the sort who enjoys her food.' If he was saying I was fat, he said it with a smile and a twinkle in his eye, so, hungry or not, I polished off the lot.

Once he'd eaten he was anxious to talk. Mostly about his father. 'I know you're only trying to help a friend but it's fired up my dad's obsession. He's out now seeing a chap in Devon who he used to work with years back. I tell him he's wasting his time but he doesn't listen.'

As I listened to him I began to wonder about Liam. Without any real justification at all I had the feeling that he wanted his father to stop trying to nail Warrinder, for reasons other than health. 'What are you worried about most?' I asked. 'Your dad getting sick, or are you trying to hide something from him?'

'What the hell are you talking about?' The twinkle had gone from his eyes, to be replaced by an angry glint. Here goes another potential romance, I thought. When would I learn to keep my mouth shut? 'I only meant that perhaps you're trying to protect your dad by not letting him know all the facts.'

'What facts?'

'Well, it seems the drugs scene is flourishing in Cornwall, Newquay especially, and I wondered if the police were ... well ... turning a blind eye.'

He stared at me. 'You're really asking about bent coppers, aren't you?'

'I suppose I am. Every force has got one or two, or so I've heard.'

'Really?' he said. 'Is that what you've heard?'

Was I being that irritating or was that a touch of guilt in his voice? I couldn't be sure but I couldn't just leave it there. 'I've read about huge hauls of cannabis and cocaine,' I said. 'What happens to it?'

'Everything we find is dealt with by the civilian property officer, logged in and sealed with a number and date. Not only is the item manually accounted for but it's also put on computer.'

'And who destroys it?'

'It varies.'

He was being deliberately evasive. The temptation would be as great as if pound notes were about to be destroyed. Some would succumb. And I was beginning to wonder if he was one who would. Liam stared at me for a moment then smiled. 'I reckon you're in the right line of work after all.'

'That's good,' I said. 'Cos I'm stuck with it.'

'Rest assured,' he said, 'that everything is done to ensure that any drugs do not leave the property office until the court case, when they may be produced as evidence. The court then passes a Drugs and Paraphernalia Order so that the drugs may be destroyed.'

'And the destruction?'

'That takes place at local headquarters. The drugs are incinerated in the presence of a senior officer not below the rank of super-intendent. Satisfied?'

'Yes ... but...'

'But what?'

'The drugs could still be siphoned off at source. A little bit here, a little bit there, even before getting to a police station.'

'Yes, and the chief constable might be a pole dancer. Let's get off this subject, Kate, before I get really irritated.'

Fair enough, I thought, and changed the subject. 'What plans has your dad in mind for nailing Warrinder?' I asked.

Liam shrugged. 'He knows I'm the voice of caution but he also knows he can take more risks than I can, because he's no longer in the force. I'm sure he thinks he won't be prosecuted – but he will if they find out.'

'For what?'

'Skulking around Tamberlake. He's had keys to that place for ages.'

'So, he still thinks Alison is buried there?'

'Oh yes. Nothing, bar a severe hammering, will shift that idea from his head.'

'Maybe he needs some help.'

'You're thinking of going there with a pickaxe and a shovel are you?'

'No, but tomorrow I'm planning to see Helen and if everything goes according to plan I'm going to meet Paul Warrinder – see what I make of him.'

Liam sat back in his chair grinning.

'What's so funny?' I asked.

'It's just that you seem to think a bit of feminine intuition will crack the case like an elephant stamping on a walnut.'

'I do not! But it's best to know the enemy. Meeting him would be a help. Then at least I'd know what we were up against.'

'He's as slippery as baby oil on smooth tiles. You won't trap him with words.'

I thought about that for a moment. 'Didn't they get Al Capone on tax evasion?'

'They did. Has Warrinder, to your knowledge, been evading tax?'

'No, but if he could be arrested on a minor charge,' I said, 'once he was in custody he could be questioned more fully.'

'Don't you think he was questioned before? We didn't use the thumbscrews but he told us nothing that would incriminate him.'

'What about the fact that it seems he

hasn't been to Argentina, and if he has, he was travelling on a false passport?'

Liam smiled. 'A false passport is an offence but lying about where you are isn't.'

I realized then I wasn't going to win any arguments with him so I simply said, 'I still need to meet him.'

'Just be very careful.'

Strange, I thought, how contrary is human nature. The more you are exhorted to 'be careful', the more exciting the risk seems.

I left on a cheerful note, with Liam promising to ring me and fix up a proper dinner date. 'On one proviso,' he said. 'No shop talk. We talk trivia.'

'I can do trivia,' I said. He opened the car door and then kissed me full on the lips. Not bad, I thought. Not bad at all.

I was driving away feeling exceptionally cheerful when my mobile rang. I parked the car and rummaged in my bag. It was Helen.

'Kate. I hear you're in Cornwall. Paul's back. He's been a bit naughty – he came back early from Argentina but he's had a stomach bug and he didn't want to burden Gill and I with his being ill, so he stayed with a friend.'

'That was thoughtful of him.'

'You really must meet him. Come for lunch tomorrow.'

'Love to.'

'About one?'

'I'm looking forward to it.'

Warrinder was indeed slippery. I didn't think he would give himself away, but someone else surely would.

I drove on to Exeter to visit Hubert. In daylight the journey didn't seem so far and I managed to find a parking space after driving around the hospital grounds a mere twice.

Hubert sat in a chair by his bed, wearing a striped hospital dressing gown. At first I thought he was asleep but then I noticed one eye was slightly open. The bruising was more pronounced now and the heroin had obviously left his system. I was impressed, though, that his tooth was back in place. He pointed to his tooth. 'Some medic fixed it,' he said. 'He told me it was superglue and I don't think he was a dentist.' I smiled and sat down. 'Don't just sit there grinning. Get me out of here, Kate. I can't stand it. I won't be getting a blanket bath and the baths here aren't clean.'

'I'm surprised you can see well enough to notice.'

'I'm serious, Kate. The hotel is cleaner, the bed's more comfortable and the food's better. I'm coming out.'

'Don't think I'll be blanket-bathing you, because I won't.'

'I wouldn't let you, you can be ham-fisted.'

'I'd butter me up if you want to get out

of here.'

He stood up unsteadily.

'Sit down again,' I said. 'You'll have to sign a form first.' He sat down again like a sulky schoolboy and I went off to find the nurse in charge. I found her in the nurses' station looking frazzled. Her attitude suggested that, as long as Hubert signed the appropriate forms, he could crawl out on all fours. He was just one less for her to worry about.

When I returned Hubert was waiting by the door wearing his own bloodstained clothes. In fact he was holding on to the door. I realized guiltily that I'd been too preoccupied to remember he might have needed clothes and toiletries. He grabbed the forms, I provided a pen and he signed them using the doorframe to rest them on. On the way out I handed them in at the nurses' station to be countersigned and then the frazzled ward sister managed a tight smile. 'Any problems,' she said, 'see a GP as a temporary resident.' In other words never darken our doorstep again. I thanked her, Hubert muttered his thanks and then, with him hanging on to my arm, we made our way slowly out of the hospital.

Once in the car, Hubert murmured that he felt very weak and within a mile or so of the hospital his head had slumped forward and he was asleep and snoring.

Back at the Regis, as I helped Hubert into

reception, Jimmy the porter rushed forward to help support him, as his legs didn't seem to be responding. We managed between us to get him to his room, where the porter helped him on to the bed and removed his jacket and trousers. Hubert's white vest was blood-stained, so between us we removed that and slipped on his blue silk pyjama top. 'What a poser,' I said. Hubert grunted but obviously didn't appreciate the comment. After Jimmy the porter had left I went next door and released Jasper.

When he saw Hubert he barked and circled and his whole body quivered with joy. Then he managed to scrabble on to the bed and snuggle down beside him. Hubert raised a languid hand and stroked Jasper's head. A few minutes later they were both asleep and even the hotel manager's knock at the door didn't wake them.

'How is he?' he whispered as he peered in on the sleeping duo.

'He'll be fine now he's back here.'

'What would he like for dinner? Chef can rustle up anything your dad fancies.'

'Perhaps some grilled plaice and mashed potatoes?'

'No problem. Soup? Dessert?'

'He likes jelly and ice cream and tomato soup.'

'Fine. Anything you need, just let me know.'

I thanked him profusely and he gave me an old-fashioned bow and left.

As I closed the door I thought Hubert was right. The Regis Hotel was a better bet on the healing stakes. Hospital was fine if you were unconscious and unable to worry about hygiene shortcomings, the awful food, the noise and the lack of fresh air. In his own room Hubert could have peace and quiet and Jasper to aid his recovery.

By the time Hubert's dinner tray arrived he'd slept for three hours. A young waitress brought up the tray and gazed at Hubert asleep with his mouth wide open. 'Bless him,' she murmured as she placed the tray on the coffee table.

As she closed the door Hubert woke and with his half open eye spied the tray. 'You go down to the dining room and eat. If you think you're going to sit here and watch me eat you can think again.'

'If you're sure you can manage...' I began. He didn't let me finish, he just waved me away, so I sloped off to the dining room desperately hoping that Beatrice and Franklin wouldn't decide to keep me company. They did. And they wanted to know all about Hubert's attack. I half expected them to ask about the state of Hubert's bowels but they didn't go quite that far. Having established that the police had a name and description of the assailants, I was then subjected to a discourse, during my main meal, on the American judicial system and its superiority. Franklin believed that capital punishment was the only answer to every crime from mugging to murder. He was so bellicose and convinced he was right, I merely listened and vowed to have meals in my room from now on. I soon grew so tired of his pontificating that I declined dessert, saying I had to check on Hubert.

I found him sitting out in his blue silk pyjamas looking more chipper. 'I was starving,' he said. 'I feel so much better now. I can think clearly again.'

I knew Hubert well enough to know that he had an idea, but he thought his ideas were solutions and I hoped his 'clear thinking' wasn't another scheme that should be kept locked in the labyrinthine depths of his mind.

'London,' he said.

'What about London?'

'We shouldn't be here in Cornwall. The answer is in London.'

'What answer?' I asked.

'Whatever Warrinder is up to – he's not doing it in Cornwall.'

Nineteen

That night I sat propped up in bed watching television but unable to concentrate. Maybe the answers were in London and not Cornwall but at the moment there were more loose ends locally. Loose ends! Who was I kidding? We'd achieved nothing between us. Hubert's beating and a dose of heroin were hardly an achievement. In a week I'd managed to find out that Warrinder either had a false passport or he hadn't been to Argentina at all, also that their friends had lied about the night Fran supposedly committed suicide, and that was the sum total of actual knowledge. I lay awake for hours trying to plan some sort of strategy but apart from getting Hubert safely back home the rest was a blur.

The next day Hubert's eyes were virtually open but he didn't have much energy and seemed to be content to lie in bed watching television and waiting for his meals to be delivered. I rang my mother, Marilyn, and she told me, with a hint of *I told you so* that David and Megan were 'getting serious'. I told her I was pleased but I don't think she believed me. She'd had a taste of surrogate grandmotherhood and now the great wide world was beckoning her. Her latest venture, she informed me, was to buy a camper van and 'see Europe'. I doubted Europe wanted to see her, and I wondered how someone who was always broke could afford a camper van, and I guessed some fool bank manager had given her a loan. But I didn't ask. I did ask about my god-daughter Katy, who it seems is 'a little peach'.

Hubert is occasionally psychic and just before I was about to leave for lunch at Tamberlake he looked up from the television and stared at me for a few moments.

'You've been talking to your mother.'

'How can you tell that?'

'A look comes over your face,' he said.

'Worried? Anxious?'

'No,' he said, shaking his head. 'Mystified. Like you've seen the ghost of things to come and you don't like it.'

'My mother is such an airhead she—'

'Just be grateful you've got a mother. She is an airhead but given half a chance you would be too. And she's not good at choosing men, so you do have that in common.'

'Are you trying to depress me?'

'No,' he said, trying to look the innocent.

I changed the subject before I did get depressed. 'I'm off to see Helen at Tamberlake. She's cooking lunch. You'll be all right on your own – won't you?'

'Jasper's here,' he said. 'We'll be fine.' Jasper awoke from sleep, nuzzled Hubert's hand and wagged his tail. I was surplus to requirements.

I arrived at Tamberlake as the looming black clouds decided to shed their cargo of rain, and in the few seconds it took me to reach the front door I was soaked. I hadn't worn a coat, just a long summer skirt and a white blouse. They clung damply to me as I waited for someone to answer the front door.

It was Paul Warrinder who answered the door. He was better-looking in the flesh than in photographs. His smile was warm, his teeth perfect. His eyes, although dark, almost black, reminded me of pools of petrol, with those shiny flecks of colour in them.

'Come on in,' he said. 'You look as if you need to dry off.' He guided me to the down-stairs cloakroom, where I towel-dried my hair and dabbed at my clothes.

Helen was there to greet me when I came out. 'It's good to see you again, Kate. I thought after the trouble with Gill you might not speak to me again.' She didn't give me time to reply, before suggesting we had a glass of wine in the sitting room. 'Don't worry about Paul, he's in the kitchen pre-paring lunch. He's making pizzas.'

'From scratch?'

'Yes. He's a great cook and he loves it, so I just leave him to it.'

Helen poured out the Argentinian wine. 'I have to explain to you,' she said, 'about how I met Paul. I did meet him in a camera shop but it was before Fran ... died. We just chatted. After that I seemed to see him quite often, just around and about with his children. We were *not* having a relationship. I thought he was gorgeous-looking but he wasn't free and I wouldn't chase after a married man.'

'What was he buying in the camera shop?' I asked.

She frowned. 'A camera ... why do you ask?'

'I just wondered. He's keen on photography then?'

'Oh yes. That's one of the things we have in common.'

I sipped at my wine, one glass would have to last unless I was prepared to take a taxi back to the Regis and leave Hubert's car behind. Helen stared into her wine glass. 'I hope Gill and I will make up soon,' she murmured. 'I *really* want her to come to the wedding.'

Helen was far more edgy now that Paul had returned. I was about to ask her *why* when he appeared at the door to announce that lunch was ready. We dutifully followed him to the kitchen, where a mega-size pizza had just been removed from the oven. He'd also made coleslaw and provided a huge salad. If nothing else, Helen would at least be well fed. I couldn't resist another glass of wine and halfway through the meal I began to feel pleasantly mellow. So mellow that when Paul asked if I enjoyed being a private investigator I was able to say that it *had its moments*.

'Helen told me,' he said, looking me straight in the eye, 'that Gill was convinced not only had I killed Alison but that somehow I was responsible for Fran and the children's death. That was very hurtful, as you can imagine.'

I nodded. I didn't know what to say. Helen murmured, 'Paul, darling, don't let's get heavy. Gill means well.'

'I'm not getting heavy, sweetheart,' he said evenly. 'I just want to get the record straight for Kate. I've had enormous bad luck recently. It hasn't been easy, but meeting Helen has given me another crack at happiness and I don't want anything to spoil that. I'm sure you can understand that, Kate.'

I nodded again, feeling like one of those toy dogs dangling in the back of a car. In truth I was wary of putting my foot in it. The less I said, I reasoned, the more he would talk.

'I've heard via my friends,' he continued, 'that you've been asking questions about me. The latest rumour is that I'm a drug dealer and that our Saturday night dinner parties were drug-fuelled orgies and that's why Fran … did what she did.' He paused, still looking me straight in the eye. 'I'll admit I told the police that we had cancelled the dinner party that night but I did it to protect them. They knew nothing about Fran's death and they were devastated by the news. What use would it be subjecting them to police questioning when there was nothing to say?'

'That makes sense,' I said to mollify him. Then I finished the last mouthful of pizza on my plate, murmured that it was delicious and sipped at my wine. It gave me a chance to decide how to make a comment more of a question, and one that might prove illuminating. 'I can't help wondering,' I said, 'about Fran's state of mind that evening. Feminine curiosity, I suppose.'

Paul shrugged. 'Looking back, she seemed a little subdued but I wouldn't say depressed. She always looked forward to Saturday nights. It gave her a break from the cooking, because I always cooked and cleared up afterwards. She got dressed up and the children went to bed early, which gave us a chance to have a quiet drink before our friends arrived.'

'You said she was subdued – was there a

reason?'

Paul sat back in his chair and ran his hand through his hair. 'As I said, in retrospect I think poor Fran had been subdued since Josh was born. I think she had post-natal depression but she insisted it would pass and – her words – she didn't want her "emotions artificially tampered with by medication". I should have insisted earlier but I did insist in the end because she couldn't sleep at night, saying that she could hear things. I thought with medication and proper sleep she'd be OK but I was wrong. Very wrong.'

'Were you surprised she didn't leave a suicide note?'

A pained expression crossed his face. 'I don't think the word "surprise" is adequate. I was in total shock. Numb. It was as if I was walking through fog. Nothing made any sense. If you're talking about raw emotion, when the fog lifted – I was angry. Very angry. Fran had every right to kill herself, but to take my babies with her, with no explanation, was unforgivable.'

There was silence then. I could see Paul's hand trembling slightly and his eyes glimmered. It was Helen who broke the silence. 'Time for coffee,' she said quietly.

Over coffee I changed tack. 'What about Alison?' I said. 'Where do you think she's gone?'

'To be honest, I don't care,' he muttered

under his breath. Then added, 'Don't get the wrong impression. I loved her. I wanted children by her. She wanted to be free, I suppose. This house is a job in itself. I think she saw the future and didn't like what she saw. She wasn't particularly domesticated. She saw the restrictions and got out.'

'Weren't you ... a bit surprised she didn't give you an explanation?'

'There you go again,' he said, with the briefest of smiles. 'I was hurt that she couldn't talk to me. Not wanting to marry me was, of course, her choice, but we could have remained friends.'

'Would that have worked?'

He looked thoughtful. 'No. Probably not.'

'Were you ... concerned when she didn't contact her half-brother?'

He smiled. 'There you have me, Kate. This time I was surprised. They were fairly close. I have to admit it was only when Fran died that I did wonder if Alison too had killed herself or gone adrift in some out of the way country.'

'Why would she have killed herself?'

'No particular reason. But she too could be a little unstable at times.'

'But you didn't do anything to find her?'

'No. Why should I?'

Why indeed? I supposed if I was engaged to a bloke who went AWOL I wouldn't necessarily think he was a missing person –

just that he didn't want anything more to do with me. I'd have still wanted some sort of explanation, but then life doesn't always give you explanations. Life's a bitch. I guessed that was Paul's attitude too.

Helen had remained very quiet but now she'd obviously had enough of the serious stuff, because she began to bustle about, noisily clearing the table. With two of Paul's exes being supposedly 'unstable' and her afraid to be in the house on her own, I did wonder if her IQ only reached double figures, and tried to remember if she'd shown any promise at school. My abiding memory was still of her white socks and the braces on the teeth, so she hadn't shone academically, because I certainly couldn't remember ever asking to cadge a look at her homework. Was she 'unstable' too? Or was Tamberlake responsible? She refused my offer of help to stack the dishwasher but forced a smile. 'We're having our usual Saturday night dinner party tomorrow. You will come, won't you?'

'You mean the same friends that—'

She didn't let me finish. 'Of course. They're incredibly loyal, aren't they, darling?'

He stood up and put his arm around her. 'I don't know how I would have survived without them.'

Twenty

The next day Hubert had resumed life in the world of communal dining. We were given a table for two and Hubert was fussed over like a minor celebrity. Whilst I'd been at Tamberlake the previous day the police had arrived to take a statement. Big Charlie and the barman had disappeared but they were hopeful that they would be caught. I remained sceptical.

Hubert dropped his bombshell once we'd finished our mammoth breakfast. 'I'm going home,' he said. 'But don't think I've lost my nerve, just because I was nearly killed. The locum isn't coping that well and I don't want my reputation put in jeopardy.'

I stared at him and he looked away. He was scared. His brush with death had upset him more than I'd realized. 'Couldn't you hang on for one more day? I could drive you home tomorrow.'

He shook his head.

'Please think about it. You're not well enough to drive. We could go straight after breakfast tomorrow.'

Eventually he said, 'Oh all right, but I don't want you gadding off and leaving me on my own all day.'

'Fair enough,' I said. 'We'll gad together. Picnic? Pub lunch? A paddle in the sea?'

Hubert's eyes lit up. 'I haven't had a paddle in the sea for years.'

So we did just that. I ordered a packed lunch via reception and by ten thirty, Hubert, Jasper and I were driving to the beach. The sun shone thinly but promised warmth to come and after hiring a wind-breaker and two deckchairs we planned to spend the day reading the papers, eating and throwing sticks for Jasper. It took Hubert a while to get the courage to remove his socks and shoes – he doesn't own sandals – and roll up his trouser legs. He strode off to the water's edge at a brisk pace, hesitated for a few seconds then took the plunge until the sea lapped as far as his ankle bones. He paused for a few more seconds looking out to sea with a hand over his eyes, then he turned abruptly and walked back to our little camp in the sand. 'Too bloody cold,' he said gloomily.

'What did you expect for your feet – the Caribbean?'

As he picked up a towel he looked hope-fully at me, as if he'd like me to dry his feet. My eyes stayed resolutely on my newspaper. Not that my mind was on the usual array of bad news and health scares. I hadn't told him I was invited to the Saturday night soirée. It was time to broach the subject. He didn't respond at first, other than with a grunt that I interpreted as disapproval. 'I think his looks have swayed you,' he said. 'Now that you've met him and found out he can cook pizza – he must be a saint.'

'I only said I thought he *might be* telling the truth. Innocent until proved guilty and all that. But, saying that, I think that I think he's a pompous prat and, for all his posturing – as cold as the sea you've just paddled in.'

'Robert Roberts thinks there's no doubt.'

'Yes. But he's the old school of cop – convict at all costs.'

'I think he talks a lot of sense,' said Hubert, slipping his socks back on. 'And he was willing to lay his career on the line because he was convinced that Warrinder is guilty of murder.'

'Evidence of that is not forthcoming. There's something I've missed.'

'Just the one thing?'

'Warrinder bought a camera...' I tailed off. Something told me it was significant but I had no idea why. Then realization dawned. It was merely the fact that it was an *item*. Like a computer.

'I've got it!'

'What?'

'In the whole of Tamberlake, and that

includes the attic, there is no computer.'

'Don't get carried away,' said Hubert, giving me a worried glance. 'Lots of people don't have a computer.'

'Not people like Warrinder. The cleaner, Carole Jackson, she'll know if he's ever had one.'

'I'm flummoxed,' said Hubert. 'I reckon you've had too much sun.'

'No. I'm convinced this is a lead. Come on, Hubert, you've had your paddle. Let's get to work.'

In my enthusiasm I hadn't given a thought to *which* camera shop. Hubert remained flummoxed. 'So what?' he said. 'Warrinder buys a camera. Next we'll be checking out where he buys his loo paper.'

It was hard to explain why I thought it was significant. Warrinder had encroached on Fran's artwork and just by chance he meets a professional photographer. I'd thought Helen had been the one doing the chasing – now I wasn't so sure.

I'd never seen a camera shop in Trevelly, so we started on the inland towns of Bude and Launceston. In Launceston we struck lucky. There in the main street was a camera shop, its small windows crammed with every type of camera. Unfortunately I assumed the young man at the counter was a shop assistant, so that when I asked him how long he'd worked there he replied sharply that he was the owner and had been there for fifteen years. Tall and lanky, with fair cropped hair, a pale skin with no signs of crow's feet, I thought that, whatever secret he had in the youth stakes, I wished I had it too.

'I wondered if you could help us,' I began, then hesitated. I didn't want to mislead him into thinking we actually wanted to buy a camera, but he might not cooperate if we told him the truth. 'A girlfriend's fiancé bought a camera here about six months ago and he recommended it but I don't know the make.'

'What do you want it for?' he asked.

'Taking photos, of course.'

'No, I meant for holiday snaps or more impressive, professional stuff?'

'My friend is a professional photographer – it's a wedding present. So we'd like the same one.'

'Name of buyer?'

'Paul Warrinder.'

'Hang on. I'll look through my records.'

He disappeared into a back room and Hubert began browsing amongst the glass-encased cameras.

Within a few minutes he was back with a sales docket. 'That was easy enough,' he said. 'Thought I recognized the name. He's been in a couple of times.' Then he added with a slight frown, 'It's an expensive one. But it wasn't a camera – it was a Sony camcorder – nine hundred pounds worth.'

Now I really was lost for words but Hubert came to my rescue. 'I think we'll just have a middle-of-the-range camera,' he said, pointing to one in the glass case underneath the counter. 'Good choice,' said the owner. 'Takes a fair photo does that one.'

Hubert paid on his credit card and, as we walked out into the street, muttered, 'I've never owned a good camera before.'

'Well aren't you the lucky boy,' I said, feeling peeved that I wasn't any wiser now that I knew Warrinder had bought a camcorder. So what? I was more interested in his lack of a computer. Perhaps he had a computer somewhere else or he'd got rid of it because it contained something incriminating – like a suicide note.

When I suggested this to Hubert he snorted, 'I've never known anyone write a suicide note on a computer.'

'It could be a new trend for the twenty-first century. People end relationships via e-mail now.'

'Very few,' he replied, unconvinced.

Back in Trevelly I drove towards Carole's place. We saw her emerging from a local shop with several plastic bags of food. She was grateful for a lift and invited us in for a cup of tea. Whilst she put her food away and Hubert admired her legs I asked her about the computer. 'When Fran was alive,' she

234

said, 'he had one in the study upstairs.'

'You mean the attic?'

'Yeah. I only went in there once a month to give it a bit of a dust. He was tidy.'

'And after she died?'

'That was when he took to keeping it locked. I thought he'd put all their belongings up there – toys, photos, clothes, that sort of thing. He cleared the house of their personal stuff about a week after they died. Didn't want to be reminded, I suppose.'

'So, you don't know what happened to the computer?'

'No idea, love. Is it important?'

'Could be. I'm not sure. What about a camera? Did he have a camera?'

'He did. He was always taking photos. He took a real pride in it.'

'You don't know where he had the films developed?'

She sat down wearily on a kitchen stool and crossed her legs. She was wearing a short denim skirt and mules with a slight heel. The view kept Hubert dumbstruck. 'I don't know where he went,' she said slowly, 'but she used a shop in Newquay – one of those gift shops, I think, that do other things on the side.'

As Carole looked so tired, I didn't want to outstay our welcome. 'Just one more question,' I said. It was one of those little niggles that had been troubling me. 'How often exactly would you say Paul went away?'

'I can tell you that. Every month while Fran was alive. That was the week I did the attic.'

'Did he always go abroad?'

'Mostly, I think. I did once joke to Fran that maybe he was a spy...' She hesitated. 'Look, I may as well tell you ... when I was up in the attic I did have a nose round. Not that there was much to find, but one day I did find a card with an address scrawled on the back. I remember thinking that perhaps he wasn't always working ... if you know what I mean?'

I nodded. 'You couldn't by any chance remember that address?'

She put her head on one side and rested her hand on her face. 'It was London, Kensington. A flat.' Well that narrowed it down, I thought. She closed her eyes. 'Something Mews ... a herb.' I waited. 'I've got it – Rosemary Mews.'

'And the number?'

She shook her head, still with her eyes closed. 'I think ... I can't be sure, it was either eight or three.'

'You are a genius,' I said delightedly. 'Thanks so much.'

'Lovely woman,' said Hubert as we got back in the car.

'Lovely clever woman,' I said as we drove away.

My mobile phone trilled as we approached the Regis car park. 'Is that Kate Kinsella?' a male voice enquired. 'You don't know me, my name's Bernard.'

'Gill's boyfriend?'

Silence.

'I have some bad news. I got your number from Gill's diary...'

I felt my mouth dry. 'What's happened?'

'Gill was involved in an accident two days ago. Early this morning they switched off the life-support machine and I'm sorry to say that she died half an hour later.'

Twenty-One

I tried to speak but my brain and mouth seemed one big void. Not Gill, I thought. It couldn't be true. It didn't seem possible. 'An accident?' I managed to croak.

'Yes. In central London. A motorbike courier knocked her down.'

'Have they got him?'

'No. He didn't stop.' Bernard's voice had a shocked robotic sound.

'I'm so sorry. I don't know what to say. She was...' I paused, about to trot out the old clichés used when someone young dies.

'I don't even know why she was there,' Bernard continued. 'There's a perfectly good gym locally but she wanted to try a more expensive one. She said she might meet some celebrities.'

'Are the police convinced it was an accident?' I asked quietly.

'You mean ... it could have been deliberate?'

'Yes. It's a possibility.'

'Oh my God!'

'I'm sorry if I've made things worse.'

'Nothing could be worse than losing her.'

'I know,' I murmured. 'I'll meet you in London. We can talk...'

'When?' he asked dully.

'Two days – Tuesday...' I paused. 'Have you told Helen yet?'

'I tried but she wasn't answering her phone.'

'Leave it to me,' I said. 'I'm seeing her tonight.'

He gave me his address and phone numbers and then, barely audibly, he said goodbye.

Hubert frowned in puzzlement. 'Gill's dead?'

I nodded. I didn't want to talk about it; I had to mull it over quietly. He patted my knee and we drove on in silence.

At nearly eight p.m. I arrived at Tamberlake, parked the car and sat for a few minutes watching the sky darken. The news of Gill's death had really shaken me and I wondered how much she had told Bernard about the situation. I dreaded the evening ahead. When would I tell Helen? Before the meal? Afterwards? She'd get no sleep whenever I told her. This was my chance to meet Paul's clique of friends, possibly my only chance. I made my decision. I would tell Helen tomorrow. And I was determined that this night would be a turning point.

Paul greeted me at the door, kissed me on both cheeks and, with an arm around me, led me to the kitchen. I was the last to arrive. He introduced me as, '*The* Midlands Sleuth, an old school friend of Helen.'

Jamie Ingrams and Harvey Trenchard sat between two women, the elusive Michelle Ford and Diane Brandon. Michelle was a redhead in her forties wearing jeans and a black low-cut top. She was striking rather than attractive – her long nose and thin face was saved from severity by soft blue eyes. Diane in contrast had neat features but small grey eyes. She wore a long brown skirt and a cream top. She was Miss Average in looks and below average in friendliness. She stared at me and didn't respond to my cheerful hello. I guessed she was in her late thirties and I couldn't help finding it strange that not one of the four seemed to have a partner.

Trenchard stared at me too and murmured something to Diane, whose little grey eyes darted briefly over my body like a shop assistant deciding dress size at a glance. Paul began pouring wine. Helen checked the oven and then placed a basket of French bread and a bowl of salad on the table. Michelle smiled at me. 'What exactly are you investigating in Cornwall? Rumours are abounding, I can tell you – everything from drug dealing to Satanism.'

'I'm just ghost-busting and catching up

with old friends.' I glanced at Helen, who'd sat down to await Paul's triumphant offering from the oven. Surprisingly she winked at me. 'I'm sure Helen's told you the full story,' I said, hoping she was going to help me out.

'I have,' she answered. 'I've told them I think this place is haunted and Jamie's extremely worried about the whereabouts of his half-sister.'

Michelle, far from being sympathetic, laughed. 'Jamie, you know your half-sister was slightly eccentric. She'll turn up.'

'Why do you say she was eccentric?' I asked.

Before she could answer, Jamie angrily snapped a piece of French bread in half. 'Kate, take no notice,' he said. 'Michelle is a frustrated old bag who hasn't had a man since 1990.'

'And you are an old queen who hasn't had a man ... not a proper man ... ever!'

'You two,' said Paul as he put on oven gloves, 'are like bickering four-year-olds. Take no notice, Kate, they just do it for effect.'

Paul served his Italian chicken dish, strong on garlic, tomatoes and basil, and the conversation turned to cars, holidays and the forthcoming wedding. It was Diane who first mentioned Fran. She'd been drinking wine steadily and far from being merely unfriendly I realized that she'd been getting

241

maudlin drunk. 'It was this time last year that Fran—'

'Drop it!' snapped Trenchard.

'No I won't! Fran and the kids were my friends. I'm not going to pretend they didn't exist. Paul might be able to do that but I can't.'

Paul winced slightly. 'Life goes on. I couldn't grieve for ever.'

'Since when has a mere six months been for ever?'

Helen now looked uncomfortable and she stopped eating and began pushing the food around her plate. Paul placed a hand over hers and Helen tried to smile. 'Don't deny me happiness, Diane. I never thought I'd feel like this again.'

Diane's answering smile was more of a sneer. 'You said exactly that after Alison had left and you met Fran.'

He shrugged. 'I can't help it if love came knocking once more.'

I looked over to Helen, who I expected to be a little upset by all this, but she merely smiled at me and began clearing the used plates. 'I think,' said Paul, 'we should have a special bottle of wine tonight.' There was a murmur of agreement, or maybe relief that the conversation had ended.

As he went to the cellar, Diane looked at her wristwatch. 'Last year at this time Fran went down to the cellar seeming fine. She came back, pale and shaking, saying she felt a bit faint. Strange how much Paul drank from then on. He was drinking whisky when usually he sticks to wine.'

'Maybe he was worried about her,' said Trenchard. 'You really do have a nasty suspicious mind.'

'You wouldn't notice if your own socks were on fire,' said Michelle.

Trenchard laughed. 'I'm never quite that pissed.'

'You were that night,' retorted Michelle.

'Was I? I don't remember.'

'I remember. We all drank too much...'

'We usually do,' he interrupted, 'and don't forget we were on the spliff as well.'

Michelle didn't answer but Diane, looking furious, snapped, 'Which is why we were told to keep our mouths shut and deny we were ever here.'

'Paul was only trying to protect us all,' said Trenchard. 'Don't forget I drove home that night.'

'Yes, and God knows how we got away with that,' said Diane. 'We could easily have been seen.'

Trenchard shrugged. 'It was late. Most of Trevelly is asleep by ten thirty.'

'Anyway, I was talking about Fran...'

At that moment Paul walked back in, carrying two bottles of wine, and, after a short silence punctuated only by the sound of popping corks, he poured the wine into fresh glasses. He was handing the glasses round when Diane looked at me and cocked her head towards the door. 'Excuse me, Paul,' she said. 'I need to throw up.' She left the room and a few seconds later I followed, saying, 'I'll just check on Diane.'

I saw her at the open cellar door, obviously waiting for me. As I approached she said quietly, 'I'm not stupid and I'm not even that imaginative but I'm sure Fran found something in the cellar that night.'

'But she was hearing things more than seeing them, wasn't she?'

'If she'd heard something she would have told us. I'm sure she saw something. She came back into the kitchen and she was scared. When I heard she'd committed suicide I wasn't that surprised, but I was surprised about the children.'

'What on earth could have frightened her in the cellar?'

Diane shook her head. 'I wish I knew. I've been down there and I couldn't see anything ... scary.'

'Has it got a history?'

'Nothing I've heard of. It wasn't built over a burial site, so she didn't see the walking dead.' Then she touched my arm. 'Come on,' she said. 'I'm full of Dutch courage. Come down with me.'

She flicked on the light at the top of the

stairs and we walked carefully down the steep steps to the main body of the cellar. 'That night,' I asked, 'why *did* Fran come down here? Was it just for another bottle of Vin Ordinaire or was it something a bit more special?'

'Just stocking up on the cheap stuff. We were all knocking it back a bit.'

I started having a look round but since I didn't know what I was looking for it seemed a bit pointless. The one overhead light bulb didn't provide much light and I was about to suggest we were wasting our time when there was a click as the light was switched off and the door above closed. From dim light to complete dark was a shock.

'Where are you, Diane?' I asked, arms outstretched like antennae.

'Over here.'

I followed the sound of her voice and we grabbed hands and stepped towards what we hoped was the direction of the stairs. Disorientated, we took a little time to find the bottom step. Like two old grannies we began walking up the stairs. Halfway up we heard the key turn in the lock.

Twenty-Two

Sometimes only one word will do. We both began screaming 'Help!' in unison. It was mere seconds later that the light was flicked on and the door opened. Helen stood at the top of the stairs. 'I've been looking for you two upstairs.' She sounded like a mother looking for two unruly teenagers.

'Did *you* switch the light off?' I asked.

'No. It was probably Paul.'

I swore under my breath and we went back to the kitchen. 'You locked the girls in the cellar, Paul,' said Helen mildly.

'Did I? I thought you were in the bathroom,' he said. 'I passed by the cellar and I guessed I must have left the light on, so I turned it off and locked the door. Sorry.' He flashed a quick boyish grin towards Diane and me. Diane sat down, dragging her chair noisily on the tiled floor.

I sat down too, hoping at some point we'd move to somewhere more comfortable, but it seemed less likely now. Michelle looked a little glassy-eyed, Trenchard was talking about the housing market to no one in particular, Jamie followed Paul's every move and Diane had slunk into a depressive state and was staring into her glass of wine. Only Helen seemed calm and sober. Paul had a smug self-satisfied look on his face, as though he was watching the plebs from some seat of majesty. I obviously didn't know him, but on our short acquaintance I had summed him up – he was shallow, devious and cold. Everything he said was so plausible and yet ... my thoughts were interrupted by a sudden urge to get away. I needed to see Helen alone and, if I made my getaway now, Paul would wave me off at the door.

When there was a lull in the conversation I asked Paul to recommend a minicab firm. 'I'll ring them for you, Kate,' he said. 'What time?'

'As soon as possible. I've got an early start in the morning.'

He left the kitchen then, presumably to use the landline, and I moved and sat by Helen and whispered to her, 'Ring me tomorrow. I have to speak to you privately.'

'What about?'

'Gill.'

Then she really surprised me. She whispered back, 'Come here at ten o'clock. Paul should be out by then. He's going into Exeter.' I glanced around the table; no one seemed interested in the two of us together in a huddle. I nodded to her, just as Paul came back.

'Twenty minutes,' he said cheerfully. 'Time enough for a brandy.'

In the minicab on the way back to the Regis I realized that I hadn't found out who was the last to leave Tamberlake on that Saturday night a year ago. Trenchard said he'd driven home but was he alone and was he the last to leave? Was Paul indeed the last person to see Fran that night?

Hubert seemed preoccupied in the morning with phoning Humberstone's and getting back to 'normal life', if undertaking could be called normal. I left him at the hotel and drove out to Tamberlake. There was no sign of Paul and only Helen's car was in the drive.

She met me at the front door looking cheerful and I felt almost traitorous to be bringing her bad news. As she produced a cup of coffee I debated with myself how best to tell her. She sat down and stared at me. 'What is it, Kate? What's happened?'

'It's Gill,' I said. 'There's been an accident. A road accident ... I'm very sorry ... she died in hospital.'

The colour drained from Helen's face, I grabbed her hand and, although she was dry-eyed, she'd begun to tremble. 'What happened?' she asked.

'She was hit by a motorbike courier...'

'And he didn't stop?'

'That's right.'

'Where?'

'In London.'

'Where in London?'

I stared at Helen. This wasn't the Helen I thought I'd got to know. Her voice had a steely quality. I'd expected tears but not this cool interrogation style. 'Where?' she repeated.

'In Soho. She'd been to a gym.'

'The Health and Fitness Palace.'

'Yes. How did you...'

She looked at me, disengaged her hand and said, 'I can't tell you anything, Kate. You'll just have to trust me.'

I couldn't help it. I stared at her. The new Helen wasn't the timid, slightly dull bride-to-be I'd thought she was. From the far reaches of my memory I had a flash of a school 'do'; friends, parents, all packed into the hall for the school play. I wasn't involved, being unable to act, but Helen had played Lady Macbeth. I'd managed to slip out during the performance and slip back in for the final curtain. There was more to Helen's past than her white socks, but what the hell was she up to now?

'I want you to help me search the cellar,' she said.

'It's been searched already.'

'Who by?' she asked.

'The police had a quick look round and

249

Robert Roberts has had a good snoop.'

There was no surprise in her expression at his name. 'His eyesight isn't too good,' she said. 'I want us to go down there with a torch and if necessary move every wine bottle.'

'That'll take some time – what if Paul comes back? And I've promised Hubert that I'll be back by eleven thirty.'

'Well we'll have to get a move on, won't we? I've got a strong torch for both of us – the light down there is useless.'

Armed with a torch each, we made our way down the cellar steps. 'You have a good look round the barrels and that corner,' she ordered. 'I'll start on the vintage stuff.'

'Fair enough,' I said. 'But what exactly are we looking for?'

'Evidence.'

'Aren't you taking pre-marital nerves a bit far?'

Even in the gloom, her answering expression said it all. She had real reservations about marrying Warrinder. 'Don't stand there with your mouth open, Kate. Let's get on with it.'

I crawled on the dusty floor; I shone my torch on individual bricks, looking for any signs of disturbance. Helen meanwhile was taking out bottles and checking the empty racks. I found some mouse droppings but otherwise not so much as a toffee paper. I was struggling up from the floor and resting my hand on one of the barrels when something glinted at me. A piece of glass, I thought, stuck in the rings. I positioned my torch at a better angle and saw it more clearly. Circular, tiny – not glass at all – but a contact lens.

Twenty-Three

'Don't touch it!' shouted Helen. 'I'll get an envelope.'

She rushed upstairs and returned in a few minutes with a pair of rubber gloves and an envelope. Delicately she removed the lens and placed it in the envelope. 'Well done, Kate. I don't know how you managed to see it.'

'What are you going to do with it?' I asked, because it was obvious she had a hidden agenda and I'd been relegated to sidekick status. Not that I minded. It was a great surprise to see Helen being proactive, but what had caused the change of heart? One moment Paul was a perfect specimen of manhood, now he was under the gravest suspicion.

'I'll take it to the Roberts' now,' she said, smiling. 'They'll know what to do.'

As we parted, she said, 'You're leaving Cornwall today?'

'I'm going to London to see Bernard, Gill's boyfriend.'

'I'll be in touch. I'll let you know about the

contact lens.'

'Was it Alison's?'

'Could be. She wore them.'

I thought it strange that Helen should know that, when no one else had mentioned it, but I supposed that maybe it was like wearing a wig, the less people who knew, the better. It was still odd that Helen should know.

I was driving away when Paul's car came into view. I smiled and waved with mock cheerfulness and after a brief surprised glance he waved back. I continued driving but I felt the urge to turn around and tell Helen to take the greatest care, because I had a gut feeling that she was in danger.

Back at the Regis Hotel, Hubert had paid the bill and was obviously keen to make his getaway. He was standing in the doorway waiting for me, with Jasper straining at the leash beside him. 'I've checked your room,' he said. 'Let's go.'

We were ten miles or so into the journey before I told him about the contact lens. 'Well done,' he said. 'I reckon a contact lens could be as good a way of identifying a body as teeth.'

'We haven't got a body.'

'Just a question of time,' he said. 'Just a question of time.'

It was early evening when we arrived back at Humberstone's. As we'd driven through

Longborough I'd noticed a new picture-framing shop. It certainly wasn't an art gallery but it did have a few paintings on easels in the front window. It seemed worth a trip and I resolved to take my two stolen watercolours there in the morning. I doubted I would get a valuation but any opinion might help. After all, what was the point of Paul trying to pass them off as his own if they were valueless?

Later that evening I rang Helen on her mobile, she didn't reply and I didn't leave a message. I rang the Roberts' home; there was no reply there either. Finally I rang Megan. My mother had left the day before – destination unknown.

In the morning I felt exhausted. I decided to take the train to London and I rang Bernard to tell him I'd meet him on Euston Station. He sounded very low and I hoped I wasn't going to make things worse for him. Death by hit and run was bad enough, but to know or suspect that it wasn't an accident, but murder, was going to be hard for him to bear.

Hubert was busy in his office downstairs, catching up on his paperwork, so I rang down on the internal phone to tell him I was going to London by train. 'In that case, take plenty of food and drink,' he said. 'You won't survive if there's a delay.'

I packed a picnic. Survival was possible but

irritability and low blood sugar were a certainty, so I took his advice ... just in case.

Before going to the station I decided to visit the art shop. It wasn't open by nine a.m. and I was about to walk away when a middle-aged woman, with plaited hair, wearing a long floral skirt and a green puff-sleeved blouse, emerged from an elderly Beetle car, produced a set of keys and opened the shop door. 'Come in,' she said cheerfully. 'You are a customer, I suppose, and not a bailiff?'

'I'm not exactly a customer but I would like some advice ... if you can spare the time.'

'Time is on my side,' she said. 'Customers are thin on the ground. Yesterday not a single soul passed my threshold. I tell a lie – the postman came delivering yet more bills.' She placed the plastic bag she was carrying behind the counter and said, 'Now, how can I help?' I took the two watercolours from my holdall, giving her the one signed by Fran first. 'I wondered if you thought this was any good.'

She gazed at the painting for a few moments. 'Not bad, fine use of light, quite delicate. I like it. Pity it's a copy.'

'A copy?' I queried in surprise.

'Yes. It's not an original.'

'Are you sure?'

'I'll check but I'm sure.'

She began taking the back apart, removing

the thick card that held the painting in place. 'What on earth...?' She paused, for underneath the card were several tiny flat packets wrapped in opaque cellophane. She stared at me. 'You look surprised,' she said, handing me the collection that had been pressed between one piece of card and another. She removed the second piece of card to reveal the painting. 'Yes, it is a copy,' she said. 'But I could probably sell them for a tenner.'

I wasn't listening. I'd opened one of the tiny packets. They were negatives. I turned my back to her and held them up to the light. Tiny images of children. Children who'd been torn from innocence into a perverted adult world. Each negative had some sort of number code in the corner and each child had a name. I felt sick. I'd expected Warrinder to be involved with drugs, but not this.

'Are you all right?' she asked.

I dithered for a moment. 'Yes. I'm fine. Could you put them back for me?' She fixed the packets back in place and reassembled the painting. I couldn't have managed, because my hands were trembling. 'Would you check this one out too?' I asked her, handing her the second painting. Carefully she unclipped the back. This time there was no false backing and when she examined the painting she judged it to be an original. I returned the paintings to my holdall, thanked her and left the shop.

Outside, I took several deep breaths. As I walked away I caught a glimpse of the shop owner watching me go. I wanted to rush to the police with the negatives there and then but I needed to think carefully before I did anything.

At the train station I tried to think rationally. Would I achieve anything in London when Warrinder was in Cornwall? Prejudice had blinded me to the possibility that he might be involved in paedophilia. I'd thought him too good-looking, too self-assured. I'd assumed that somehow I'd recognize a paedophile by his shifty eyes or lack of self-confidence with women. I supposed he could be a mere purveyor of child pornography rather than a paedophile himself, but either way he had no moral objections to distributing vile images of children. I presumed he was touting his negatives in photographic form because the FBI and the British police were now monitoring the Internet much more closely. Had Fran found out about his activities? It seemed likely that she had, but what had she found, something in the cellar that night? Surely if she'd found a contact lens she'd have removed it? What the cellar at Tamberlake needed was a complete forensics team. But would finding negatives of child pornography in the back of watercolours be enough evidence to force a search of the cellar? I decided that perhaps London could provide a few answers if that was where Warrinder conducted his activities.

On the train I mulled over events, trying to separate the facts from conjecture, but I felt defeat was staring me in the face. If Warrinder was into some sort of organized child pornography ring, he'd covered his tracks well. 'Mummy, Mummy!' a child screamed out from further along the train. The sound echoed in my head. Warrinder's victims would also be crying, 'Mummy, Mummy!' only there would be no answer. The child's cries strengthened my resolve. If I had to take risks then I would. The police had been following the rules and Warrinder was still able to continue his activities. But not for much longer.

The train was approaching Euston when I realized that I had only the vaguest idea of what Bernard looked like. I'd arranged to meet him at the bar on the concourse, because it gives such a good view from above.

As the train stopped and I stepped out, a middle-aged man, balding and with glasses, smiled at me. He'd decided to meet me off the train, I thought, so I stepped forward towards him, smiling back, and he walked straight past me to the elderly woman behind me.

In the packed bar, I searched and listened for a possible Bernard whilst berating myself for being so stupid. Did I think I was going to recognize him by his voice? I ordered a glass of red wine and took it to the front of the bar, where there was a seat vacant beside a young girl who looked Japanese and who appeared to be a student catching up on her note-taking. I sipped at the wine and every so often checked the main bar by craning my neck. No one seemed to be looking for me, so I presumed Bernard was expecting the train to be delayed and would arrive soon.

One wine was enough during the day, so I drank coffee after that. Two coffees drunk very slowly and an hour had slipped by. Another coffee, another half an hour.

It was becoming obvious that Bernard wasn't going to show up. There was only one thing to do, I'd have to go looking for him. I checked his address in my diary and stood up. As I reached the door, I had one last look at the customers milling around. A man standing by the bar, pint in hand, glanced at me and then looked away. He wasn't Bernard, being far too young, in his late twenties or early thirties. He wore a suit with the tie loosened. A briefcase on the floor was clamped between his feet. Remembering Hubert's theory that shoes can tell a story, I glanced at his. Black and shiny, lace-ups, they looked brand new. My one final glance at the back of his head revealed his hair was short and very neat – I had him sussed – he was a soldier on leave.

Outside on the concourse, I began walking towards the underground taxi rank. Still on alert for Bernard I paused at 'The Sox Shop' to have a final look around. Briefcase-and-black-shiny-shoes-man caught my eye but he ducked away and I told myself that I was being paranoid if I thought he was following me.

I walked briskly down the stairs and waited behind three men in the first taxi bay. After a short wait a taxi drew up, the driver wearing a white turban and an expression of stubborn resignation. I gave him the address in Gospel Oak and he grunted in response as we swept into the usual volume of heavy London traffic. At the second set of traffic lights a black cab drew alongside us and I glimpsed 'shiny shoes' obviously on the lookout for me. Obvious, because he was deliberately peering into the cab. He *was* following me.

Twenty-Four

As the taxi neared Gospel Oak I kept peering behind but, if we were still being followed, the other taxi had either stopped or re-routed.

My driver remained mute and sullen but I gave him a generous tip and expected at the very least a slight twitch of the lips in return. He merely managed a slight nod of the head.

Bernard's house was a four-storey, Edwardian house, white with potted artificial trees outside. I was ringing the bell and banging on the door when it began to rain. I stood under the porch wondering what to do. I braved the rain to check there wasn't a spare key under the pots, then ran next door hoping he was on good terms with his neighbours. It seemed he was. A white-haired elderly woman answered the door and at the mention of his name her eyes lit up. The porch sheltered me from the rain but she didn't invite me in. 'Lovely bloke,' she said warmly in a strong London accent. 'He's a real friend to me. I live here on my own, can't make the stairs anymore. Him and a friend brought my bed downstairs – I don't know what I'd do without him. That poor Gill. He's heartbroken...'

'Have you seen him today? Mrs...?' I interrupted her.

'It's Mrs Ball. Call me Alice. No, love. Saw him last night. I made him a nice pie and took it round to him about six o'clock. He brought back the dish just after seven. He said he was going down the pub.'

'Did you see him again?'

'I was pulling my curtains across about nine and he passed by with a wave.'

'I'm a friend of Gill's,' I explained. 'He was due to meet me at Euston but he didn't show up. I wondered if you had a key.'

A flicker of anxiety crossed her pale, lined face. ' 'Course I have, love. Hang on, I'll get my coat.'

She spent some time checking that she had her own key, produced an umbrella and a walking stick and we made our way slowly next door. As she opened the door she said, 'Ever so modern this place. He keeps it lovely.' Once the door was open I could see what she meant – pure white walls in the hall, with black and white prints arranged in groups. The floor was a shiny parquet and both hall lamps were white-shaded. 'Kitchen's that way,' said Alice, pointing to a closed door at the end of the hall. 'His living room is on the left.'

The living room was a further ensemble in white and black, two white leather sofas, more white lamps and an atmosphere that made a statement. To me, it revealed that this room's function was to impress others but that not a lot of living took place there.

'Is this how it always looks?' I asked Alice.

She nodded. 'Oh yes. Bernard is very particular.'

'What about Gill? Did she help choose the furnishings?'

'I don't think so, Bernard wouldn't let anyone choose for him. Anyway, she only came round about three times a week. She didn't stay the night.'

'But I thought she lived here,' I said, puzzled.

Alice gave me an old-fashioned look. 'You don't know Bernard at all, do you?'

'No. I've never met him.'

'Well, I'm not saying he didn't love Gill, because he did. He thought the world of her but he couldn't help himself.'

'In what way?'

'Well, he was gay, dear. Always bringing different men here. He couldn't find the right man. If he'd seen one a few times, he'd bring him round and introduce him to me, and some of them were lovely. I mean, you'd never know ... they weren't like nancy boys. And they were all very nice to me.'

Alice followed me into the kitchen and I

noticed that even a short walk made her breathless, so that in the kitchen she had to sit down. The kitchen too was in monochrome, alleviated by some stainless steel. I left Alice catching her breath while I went upstairs.

I found him in bed. Lying tidily under a black duvet, head on a white silk pillow. An empty bottle of vodka and an empty packet of tablets for lowering blood pressure sat on his bedside table. A trickle of vomit had escaped from his blue mouth and it was obvious he'd been dead for some hours – the hours I'd been on the train. I guessed he'd been drinking and taking the tablets at the time I'd phoned him.

I didn't rush to ring for the police. First I had to get Alice out of the house. In the kitchen she sat looking slightly bemused, as if she'd forgotten why she was there, but if she noticed any change in my expression she didn't comment on it. 'I've never been upstairs. Same as down here, is it?'

'Yes,' I said. 'Just as tidy. Come on, let's get back to your place.'

I had to help her to her feet from the scoop-shaped chair. 'I bet he's at the undertaker's arranging Gill's funeral,' she said. I stayed silent as she added, 'That's where you'll find him.'

In Alice's living room I helped her take off her coat. 'I'm only eighty-eight,' she said, trying to catch her breath, 'but I feel at least a hundred today.'

'Do you fancy a cup of tea?' I asked.

'That would be lovely, dear,' she said.

I was relieved to be in the kitchen and have a chance to think. If I waited for the police there would be all sorts of questions. Before I knew it I'd have blurted out words like murder and paedophilia and I'd probably be locked in a padded cell. On the other hand Alice needed to know something might be amiss. Elderly and frail, she relied on Bernard for a feeling of security. I had to find out if there was anyone else she could rely on.

'Alice,' I said as I came back in with a tray of tea and the biscuit barrel. 'Have you got any friends or relatives nearby?'

'There's Maggie round the corner,' she said. 'She's younger than me but not that steady on her feet. She pops in once a week.'

I poured the tea and she was giving me a funny look. 'What have I done?' I asked. 'Don't you take milk in your tea?'

'It's not that,' she said. 'There's no biscuits in that barrel. Don't you know people keep money in biscuit barrels? Anyway, it's not airtight, biscuits go soggy in there.'

'Wouldn't burglars know you kept money in there?'

She glanced at me as if I should have more sense. 'I'd tell 'em where my money was.

Nowadays you can't win. If I clobbered him I'd go to prison and if he clobbered me he'd probably never be caught and if he was and he said he was sorry he'd be let off because the prisons are too full.' She paused, took a deep breath and fell silent.

I stared at the biscuit barrel. *Don't you know people keep money in biscuit barrels?* No, I didn't know. What do people keep in wooden barrels? The answer had been there all the time.

'I expect Bernard will be back soon,' said Alice.

'I think something may have happened to him,' I said.

I took her hand and she must have seen the anxiety in my eyes. 'He was in the house, wasn't he?' she asked. She didn't wait for my reply. 'I knew he hadn't gone out. My hearing is still good and I would have heard him.'

'I want you to ring Maggie now and ask her to come round. I'll wait here till she arrives.'

I tapped out the number she gave me on my mobile and handed it to her. She stared at the mobile phone nervously and then shouted loudly into it. 'Hello, Maggie. It's me. Could you come round? There's been a bit of bother.' Alice listened intently to the reply. 'She'll be about ten minutes,' she said. 'Her false teeth are in soak. That's a joke, they're always in soak. She only puts them in for special occasions.'

We drank tea in silence and then Alice said, 'Killed himself, did he?' I nodded. 'Did he leave a note?' she asked.

'I didn't see one but I didn't have a proper look round.'

'I bet he did. He was very organized.'

'I've got a confession to make,' I said. 'I haven't rung the police yet.'

'Nothing they can do, is there? Not now.'

'I haven't called them yet because I ... don't want to get involved.'

'You too busy?' she asked sharply.

'It's not that, I'm a private investigator and I'm on a case.'

Alice gave a sharp intake of breath. 'Well, well, fancy that. You're not investigating Bernard are you?'

'No. I was at school with Gill.'

Alice stared into space for a while and I could see it was dawning on her that Bernard really was dead. Her eyes became teary and she rubbed her hands together as though she felt cold. 'Alice,' I said. 'I want you to be brave and ring the police. Explain Bernard hasn't left the house but you let yourself in and you couldn't get up the stairs but he's not answering. You think he may be dead.'

'I bet they don't come.'

'I'm sure they will but I'd rather you didn't mention me at all. I'll give you my mobile phone number. Any problems – ring me.'

On a page from my notepad I wrote out my number in bold and handed it to her. She looked at it sadly. 'But I haven't got a mobile phone.'

'Just ring on your own telephone.'

'Oh,' she said. 'I didn't know you could do that.'

I heard the front door open and Maggie, a thin bird-like woman, walked in hurriedly, taking off her wet coat and plastic hood as she did so. I wasn't surprised she didn't wear her false teeth very often, they seemed too large for her small mouth and they moved as she spoke. She glanced suspiciously at me. 'What's up?' she asked Alice.

I saw this as my opportunity to leave. Maggie looked the determined type and I could imagine her trying to stop me leaving. 'I'll be off then, Alice,' I said. 'Remember what I said. Any problems with the police – ring me.'

'You'll come again, won't you?'

I nodded, smiled at Maggie – who scowled in response – and left.

Outside, the rain hit the pavements and the street was deserted. I'd wanted to get away but now I wasn't sure what to do or where to go next. After a minute in heavy rain I realized finding shelter in the nearest tube station was my best option. But finding that tube station proved difficult and a small hotel, the Haven, on the corner of Alice's road tempted me. Partly because I needed a haven and partly because the flashing neon vacancy sign caught my eye. It was more a B&B than a hotel but at least it would be dry and from there I might be able to see if and when the police arrived.

Inside, it smelt of damp overlaid with air freshener but the proprietor, a rotund man called Derek Benson cheered me up with a ready smile. 'Come on sweetheart,' he said, picking up my holdall. 'I'll show you one of our best rooms.'

Upstairs the room he offered me was large, clean, with an en suite shower and loo. 'We don't do evening meals, love,' he said. 'Breakfast is between six thirty and eight thirty. How many nights?'

'Two – maybe more. Would that be all right?'

'That's fine. No problem. There's a couple of pubs that serve food nearby, but if you don't fancy going out in the rain then I can do you sandwiches and soup. Nothing fancy – ham, cheese, cheese and onion, cheese and pickle, corned beef with or without pickle, egg, egg and cress, egg and tomato...'

I laughed. 'I get the picture. Egg and cress sandwiches please. And soup – tomato?'

He grinned. 'Yeah. We do tomato.'

Once he'd gone, promising me sandwiches in fifteen minutes, I had a quick shower and then rang Hubert. I didn't tell him about Bernard, just that I was staying at the Haven Hotel in Gospel Oak and that everything was fine. I got the impression he didn't want to talk, although he did tell me the death rate was up and he was extremely busy. I also rang Helen but there was no reply. I didn't leave a message, after all, telling her Bernard was dead was hardly likely to raise her spirits. It did occur to me that, now she suspected Paul was involved in some sort of crime, she might do a runner. If she'd known he was involved in paedophilia, she would have been out of Tamberlake faster than a pro's tennis ball.

Only a few minutes late, Derek produced my supper on a tray. The plate of sandwiches rose volcano-like on the plate but I'd eaten nothing for hours and, although the egg and cress palled after a while, I ate them all. Then I stood at the front window watching and listening for the police. Just after nine I rang Alice. She sounded tearful, the police had been. 'Everybody's been tramping in and out. They've taken my poor Bernard away.'

'I'm sorry,' I murmured, at a loss for something to say. 'But it was what he wanted.'

'Bless him,' she said sadly. 'He was only forty-five. He'd got years in front of him. I didn't think he was the type.'

I couldn't answer that. After all, I hadn't even known he was homosexual.

Next morning after breakfast I rang for a minicab to take me to the address in South Kensington. I assumed Warrinder might have stayed there or, if not, someone there might have known him.

The rain had stopped, the sun shone thinly and the driver didn't stop either talking or shouting abuse at other drivers. We had one or two near misses and by the time we arrived in the less than fashionable part of South Kensington my nerves were on edge.

Rosemary Mews was set in a Georgian terrace, some of which had long since lost its grandeur. The paintwork was grey with age and the window frames had begun to rot. Dead leaves and litter accumulated near the front door and the panel of apartment numbers had been vandalized, so that one edge had been lifted. The basement flat saw the worst of the rubbish, a wheelie bin had overflowed and a plastic bag had exuded its contents over the tiny patch an estate agent would call a patio. The basement was in darkness and there was no sign of life. I looked up. A light showed on the second floor.

I selected an identification card from my selection and slipped it round my neck. I looked up and down the road. A small band of camera-carrying tourists, wearing shorts and trainers regardless of age or size, were leaving a hotel opposite. I took out my mobile phone, so that I felt less conspicuous, and pretended to be making a call. I was doubtful about this venture but I told myself this is what private investigators did – lie and snoop and go up blind alleys in the hope that there would be some light at the end of the alley.

I pressed all four of the entrance buttons. And I waited. Then I tried again. Silence. Either no one was in or they weren't prepared to answer the door. I tried once more and then decided the only thing I could do was come back later.

This time I took the tube to Oxford Street and decided to spend the rest of the day window shopping and going to the cinema. I'd just walked into Marks and Spencer's when my mobile rang. It was Helen. 'Where are you?' she asked. She spoke so quietly I had trouble hearing her.

'M&S,' I replied.

'Have you been to the flat in South Ken?'

'Yes. No one was in.'

'Paul's on the move. He's coming to London to buy wine.'

'I'm going back there this evening.'

'No, don't!'

'Why not?'

There was a pause before she said, 'Thanks for calling. See you at the wedding.'

'Is he there?'

'Must go. See you. Bye.'

I hadn't really had a chance to tell her about Bernard but I didn't think it would help her to know. She'd sounded scared enough anyway.

Twenty-Five

I expected Helen to ring back but she didn't and when I tried an hour later the phone was switched off.

The day passed exceedingly slowly. I drank numerous cups of coffee, lunched in a pub, read two newspapers, completed a cross-word and still had hours to spare. Eventually I decided to visit a cinema for the first time in years. I settled for the latest *Terminator*, because I thought that at least the action would keep me awake.

By seven p.m. I was back in South Kensington and the lights in three flats were on. This time it seemed even less of a good idea but I took a deep breath and rang the basement flat bell. A man's voice answered the entryphone. 'I'm Jacky Bates,' I explained, 'from Environmental Health.'

A timid-sounding voice said, 'Not again ... I suppose you'd better come down.'

He stood in the doorway wearing a red baseball cap and grey sweatsuit. His skin also had a greyish tinge and his eyes were narrow and a watery blue. I guessed he was in his forties. I looked down at his feet, he was wearing trainers. 'Just back from a jog?' I asked cheerfully. He didn't reply. He just flicked his head towards the open door. I paused for a moment. I didn't like the look of him but, living in the basement flat, he probably saw more comings and goings than most and I judged it was worth the risk.

There was no hall, the front door leading straight into the living room. It smelt of stale cigarette smoke and damp. By the side of an unlit gas fire was a sleeping poodle in a plastic dog bed. In a cage on a stand near the window a budgerigar stood on his perch. An assortment of sagging chairs and a threadbare carpet completed the décor and, although there was a computer switched on with the screensaver swirling, there was no TV.

I produced a notebook and pen and began asking questions – name, date of birth, had he noticed any problems? His name was George Eccles, born in 1958, and there had been complaints before – cockroaches. He picked up a pair of plastic glasses from beside takeaway food containers and perched them on the end of his nose. 'Do you want a cup of tea, Miss Bates?' he asked.

'Mrs.' I said quickly. 'No tea thanks.'

'Well, I want one,' he said. 'You can have a look at the kitchen if you want. It's very clean.'

I followed him through to the kitchen, which was cluttered but wasn't a health risk. As he busied himself filling the kettle, I said, 'We had a complaint from one of the residents here about ... rats by the rubbish bins.'

'Who complained? I haven't seen any rats.'

'I can't give you a name. Tall, thirties, good-looking. I don't think he lives here permanently but when he does it appears he complains to us – not me personally – I'm new.'

George shook his head. 'From the basement I only see their shoes or their back view. There is a bloke I see occasionally that wears flash shoes.'

I tried to keep my voice neutral. 'Which flat?'

'The one above me. It's quiet usually but when he is there he has a lot of visitors. Noisy buggers.'

Once the tea was poured George wandered back into the living room. From under a pile of newspapers he produced an ashtray and rolling tobacco and began rolling a cigarette. 'Want one?' he asked. I shook my head. Once he'd skilfully rolled the cigarette I noticed how thin it was. I'd seen cigarettes rolled that thinly before, by men eking out their small tobacco allowance. Ex-prisoners.

'Do you have a job, Mr Eccles?'

George shook his head. 'Nah. I used to

work ... once. I don't miss it. I'm quite happy here with my pets.'

It was then that I turned to look at the budgie and the dog. They hadn't moved. They couldn't. They were not alive and, looking more carefully at them, they had never lived. Even more unnerving was the sound of footsteps above. I thanked him and left within seconds. I did pause at the door to say, 'I can't see any problems here, Mr Eccles, and my report will make that clear.'

He slammed the door, irritated, I think, that I had left so abruptly. I rushed up the steps and then made my way to the front door, but not before noticing that the lights were on in the ground-floor flat and the curtains closed. I stood on the doorstep and knew that there was no point in my being there any longer. Taking calculated risks was one thing, but being foolhardy was quite another. If Warrinder perceived the net was closing in, I didn't think he would hesitate to silence me. I was well worth taking out if I was all that stood in his way. I imagined a few lines at the bottom of the *Evening Standard*. '*A Private Investigator, Kate Kinsella, age 34, has now been missing in London for a week. Her landlord has offered a £10,000 reward for news of her whereabouts.*'

Dream on! I thought. I'd just taken out my mobile to ring Helen and had my back to the road when all hell broke loose. Sirens wailed, brakes screeched, shouts of 'Go–go–go!' echoed and seconds later I was felled to the ground. Completely disorientated and crushed by the weight on top of me, I felt my wrists being roughly handcuffed. 'I haven't done anything,' I screamed above the noise of shouting and footsteps thundering up and down the stairs. I was hauled to my feet and, although I noticed my 'assailant' was a cop with a huge girth, it was the ashen face of the man two cops were leading out – Jamie – that silenced me.

Then I was hurriedly frogmarched to a waiting police car, where I was bundled into the back seat to sit beside a young sour-faced female police officer whose most noticeable feature was a thin line of black hair on her top lip. 'What the hell is going on?'

'You'll find out. Think yourself lucky you're not in the van with the other smack heads.'

I looked to the 'van' – several men were being pushed in like cattle. 'I was only visiting,' I said.

'That's what they all say.'

'Do they all say they're private investigators too?'

She looked at me warily. 'Are you on a care in the community order?'

'I am not!'

'Well just shut up! You can say your piece at the station.'

I soon found that was not as easy as it seemed. For some reason we were driven to West End Central police station, which heaved with police, drunks, and assorted criminal types. Our arrival added to the chaos and even the desk sergeant looked bemused. 'Quiet!' he screamed. A brief lull descended. 'Take this new lot to the cells. I'll get them processed as soon as I can.'

As I stood there in the crush my mobile sounded. I struggled to remove it from my pocket, because of the handcuffs. 'I am entitled to one phone call,' I said. She scowled and removed it from my jacket pocket. Then she held it to my ear. It was Helen. 'I've been arrested. I'm at West End Central police station.'

'Pass the phone to an officer. I'll explain.'

I handed my mobile to my personal cop, who glowered at me as I said, 'My friend wants to confirm who I am.'

She snatched the phone and listened. Helen seemed to be giving her chapter and verse and the call was only marked by the odd 'Right', 'OK', 'I'll pass that on',' 'Yes', 'Thanks', 'Will do'. Whatever Helen had told her, it had worked. My handcuffs were immediately removed and she shouted above the noise, 'Sarge, I need a DCI in an interview room. Urgent! Like, now!'

'Interview room three,' he shouted back. I was quickly ushered through a coded door and into the calm of a long corridor. At interview room three, the door was opened for me and my PC said, 'I'm Debbie. Do you fancy a tea or a coffee?'

'I'd love a coffee.'

'Take a seat and I'll be back in a minute.'

Once I sat down I was aware of how fast my heart was beating. I took a few deep breaths and told myself I'd be out of here soon. I'd had a few surprises. The first was being floored from behind by a heavyweight cop, the second was seeing Jamie amongst those arrested, and now there was this huge change in attitude from the police. Perhaps, I surmised, PIs were held in slightly higher regard than I'd previously thought.

Debbie returned with a china mug of coffee and a tall man in his early thirties in a pale grey suit with a red tie. The suit looked expensive. He had friendly brown eyes, an easy smile and a full head of dark hair. 'I'm DCI Anthony Carson,' he said as he offered me his hand. 'I'm pleased to meet you, Kate.' His voice gave him away – expensive schooling, university, fast-tracker. Very attractive and probably married. All the 'pleased to meet you' bit had me worried. I smiled and remained mute.

'You'll be glad to know we have resumed surveillance on the house. I'm afraid there was some lack of communication between the Drug Squad and SO5.'

I relaxed back into my chair, suddenly aware of how tired I felt. What exactly was I supposed to say now?

'You look all in,' he said with a smile. 'I think the least I can do is to drive you home.'

'Hotel. The Haven in Gospel Oak.'

'Right,' he said briskly. 'When you're ready.'

'Hang on,' I said. 'There is something else. One of the men arrested at the house is a friend of Paul Warrinder. He's young-looking, slim – Jamie...'

'Thanks.' He looked towards Debbie. 'Get him separated from the rest. Make sure he's cautioned and I'll be back to interview him as and when. He can sweat it out for a few hours.'

Once outside and sitting in the car, a black BMW, I felt so comfortable that I worried I would fall asleep and then wake up feeling even worse. I tried to stay awake by asking him about the drug bust. 'Were any drugs found?' I asked.

'No idea,' he said. 'But then I'm not with the Drugs Squad.'

'Who are you with?'

'SO5.'

'And what does that mean?'

'I thought Helen would have told you.'

'What's Helen got to do with it?'

As we stopped at traffic lights, he glanced at me sharply. 'You really don't know, do you?'

'Know what?'

'That Helen is working undercover for SO5.'

My mouth opened and closed. I was surprised but angry with myself for being so stupid. I *had* noticed her change of attitude but I'd put that down to her realizing Warrinder was a criminal and wanting him to be caught.

'So what is SO5?' I asked.

Twenty-Six

'I'll tell you all about it over a meal,' he said. 'What do you fancy – Chinese, Thai, Mexican, Indian?'

'All food sounds good to me.'

'Good. I can't stand fussy women.'

I found myself liking DCI Carson more and more and resolved to find out if he was encumbered in any way.

In Belsize Park he stopped outside the Curry Garden on a yellow line, which made him seem somewhat adventurous. Or was that a warped view after being with the very proper David Todman on a few occasions?

The waiter greeted him by name and found us a table for two by the window. 'I used to live round here,' he explained. 'A grotty bedsit but it was home for a while.'

'After your divorce?'

'Yes,' he said. 'How did you know?'

'Just a guess.'

The restaurant's low hubbub of voices I found quite reassuring. They were having fun, enjoying the food and being ... normal. I felt far from normal, so much so that I asked Anthony to order for me. I felt far too drained to make a decision even about food.

He'd ordered a spicy prawn pancake to start but I could only nibble at it. I wanted to talk at that moment, not eat.

'Tell me about SO5,' I said, 'and about Helen. I still can't believe it.' He smiled and topped up my wine glass. I could still drink and the wine was already having an effect.

'Helen's one of our newest operatives,' he said. 'SO5 is an operation that's been under way covertly for eighteen months. Paedophilia isn't just about men sexually abusing children. It's big business and, where there is money to be made, someone will come out on top. And Paul Warrinder is one such Mr Big. We've been on to him for some time but have had no real evidence. We decided to put Helen in mainly because she looked like his dead wife and because she's a damn good actress and a good cop.'

I was still mystified. 'I hadn't seen Helen since school but Gill spoke as if they met regularly.'

'Yeah, well. They did meet over the years, but Helen didn't tell Gill she was in CID.'

'Why not?'

'Helen's married to one of our best under-cover men. The fewer people who knew about her the safer he was. Anyone who works undercover lives a strange half-life of lies and deceit and has very few friends outside the force. Undercover agents can't afford to trust anyone.'

'So, the forthcoming wedding was a set-up?' I said unnecessarily.

He nodded. 'We would have come up with an excuse to delay it if he hadn't been charged by the due date.'

'What about the Cornish police?'

'They don't know about our operation. The Roberts duo were a bit of a pain but they have proved useful.'

'And was poor Gill murdered?'

'Yes. We're ninety-nine per cent sure that she was.'

'Why?'

'She'd been making enquiries about Warrinder at the gym. We do have a suspect in our sights but we want Warrinder as well.'

When the main course arrived I took a deep breath and tried to look enthusiastic about it but I wasn't.

'So what happens now?'

He glanced at his watch. 'He's arriving by train any minute now. He's being followed.'

'And then what?'

'We'll arrest him at the house.'

'Have you got the evidence this time?'

'We think so. Since the FBI began checking suspect computers, the paedophile rings have had to become more ingenious – smuggling images via other means. For Warrinder that included specially made wine bottles that could take negatives in the base.' He paused. 'But, of course, that isn't what makes the most money.'

'What does?'

'The actual trafficking of children from around the world.'

'You mean for supplying paedophiles?'

'Yes. It doesn't get much publicity. The public would be sickened. When the children start to grow up and get more difficult we know they are murdered. "Snuff" movies still exist. The children are often orphans or they have been sold by their parents for what is for them a large sum of money.'

I was stunned into silence. The whole idea of selling children to be abused is so horrific that it's hard to comprehend. I didn't want to think about it but now it was head-on and I felt real hatred welling up for Warrinder and all those involved.

'Is he making vast sums of money?' I asked. 'I glanced at his bank accounts and they seemed normal.'

'Yes. He has other personas, false passports and bank accounts in foreign banks. Rich paedophiles will pay huge sums to fulfil their desire for a young child to use as a sexual plaything.'

My appetite had disappeared totally by then and when his mobile rang and it was obvious he would have to leave I breathed a sigh of relief. 'I'm sorry about this,' he said.

'I'll have to go.'

'What's happened?'

'They've lost Warrinder. They didn't even see him get off the train.'

He paid the bill and the manager offered me a 'doggie box' but I refused. Anthony drove me the short distance to the Haven Hotel, stopped the car and then kissed me briefly on the lips. 'I'll be in touch,' he said. I wasn't going to hold my breath. I liked him and that was worrying. He was obviously a driven man and his work would always be his number-one woman. He probably drank a lot and I'd been there before. Still, on this investigation I'd been kissed twice and I didn't know why. Were my pheromones in overdrive? It was hard to understand.

I put him out of my mind, sat in the hotel lounge and rang Helen's mobile. Not only did she not answer, there was no ringing tone. I tried again – still nothing.

I asked Derek in reception if he knew of any overnight coaches to Cornwall. He looked a bit concerned that I wanted to leave. 'I'll obviously pay now for the two nights, but I've had some bad news and I need to get back to Cornwall as quickly as possible.'

'I'll ring round for you,' he said, still looking concerned.

I sat in the lounge and rang Hubert to tell him I was returning to Cornwall.

'What for?' he asked bluntly. 'You'll wear

yourself out.'

'I know, but when this is over I'll be going back to my "maritals" and I promise I won't moan.'

'That'll be the day,' he said. 'You just take care. I need you back here.'

'What for?'

'Light relief.'

Derek came back to me with news that there was a coach leaving at eleven p.m. from Victoria coach station.

It took me about five minutes to pack my bag and return to the bar, where I drank a steadying brandy and ordered a minicab. Derek bustled in ten minutes later with a brown paper bag. 'A few sandwiches,' he said. 'You look a bit peaky.' Strange, I thought, how an act of kindness from a virtual stranger could make me tearful. There are more heroes than villains in the world, I told myself, and when it seems that criminals, drug dealers and paedophiles are everywhere, there are more kindly Dereks and Alices than the rest. Remembering Alice, I rang her to find out how she was coping.

'I'm not too bad, dear, thank you. Maggie's here with me at the moment and we're on the port and lemonade. She's going to stay the night...' She broke off and I heard them laughing. 'She's not legless yet but she says she's getting that way.'

The call cheered me even more and, when my minicab arrived, Derek carried my bag out for me and we gave each other a quick hug.

I arrived in Cornwall feeling exhausted. I'd dozed on the coach in short bursts only, because the student who sat next to me had been determined to tell me his life story. Thankfully he was only twenty, so it took a mere two hours, and his life had been incredibly uneventful, but politeness dictated I responded at appropriate moments.

It was grey-skied and threatening rain when I finally reached Tamberlake at mid morning. Helen's car was outside and although I knocked loudly at the front door there was no response. The back door was open and I called out, 'Helen! Helen!' several times as I went from room to room. Finally there was only the attic and the cellar left. I checked the cellar first – that was empty – then I went back up to the attic. The key was in the lock. I called out, 'Helen!' once more as I turned the key. I felt some resistance but pushed the door open.

Helen lay on the floor, her hand raised as if trying to bang on the door. She was still breathing and her mouth was moving. She whispered the same word twice before I finally understood. 'Hypo ... hypo.'

'You're diabetic?' I yelled, as if she were

deaf. She managed to nod slightly but her eyes were closed. She was semi-conscious and I prayed she still had her swallowing and cough reflex intact. 'You have to swallow – can you?' I didn't wait for an answer, I was scrabbling in my bag for some leftover chocolate and a can of fizzy drink Derek had packed into the brown paper bag. The fizzy orange drink was full of sugar. I removed the ringpull and, lifting her by the shoulders, encouraged her to drink. It trickled down her chin and she coughed once or twice. 'Don't choke,' I said. 'Just drink it!' I was aware I was panicking inside and it was beginning to show on the outside. 'Now suck the chocolate,' I said, placing a square into her mouth. I checked to see that it had dissolved before slipping in another square. Then I gave her more of the sugary fizz. It was a miracle I'd seen before. After a few minutes her eyes opened and, although she seemed to have trouble focusing, she muttered, 'Kate. That was a close call.'

'You're telling me.'

She struggled to sit up properly and I encouraged her to eat more chocolate and finish the drink. 'Well, I reckon you owe a man called Derek who owns a B&B a drink.'

She looked at me blankly and I didn't bother to explain. After a few minutes she felt well enough to stand up and I helped her downstairs, where I put the kettle on for some hot sweet tea.

Helen's colour gradually improved as she drank the tea. 'Why didn't you tell me you were a diabetic?' I asked, trying not to sound peeved. I could have added other questions about her being married and being in the police force but I didn't think it was the right time.

'I've only been a diabetic for two years,' she explained. 'I was stabbed and the doctors seem to think the shock may have affected my pancreas. I usually manage to keep my diabetes well controlled but I had less break-fast this morning ... you won't tell anyone I was hypo, will you?'

'No, of course I won't...' I paused. 'Who locked you in?'

'I don't know. I was searching the attic room again just in case I'd missed some-thing. I'd left the key in the lock. I didn't hear a thing. When I came to leave, I was locked in. If you hadn't found me I'd be dead by now.'

I finished my tea and realized that she had to know that Warrinder was still on the loose. 'They lost him at the station,' I told her.

She bit her lip. 'He's an evil bastard. And I've been sleeping with that monster for months.'

'Isn't that taking the line of duty too far?'

'I did volunteer, no one forced me. I wanted to do it. If you knew the children, if you'd heard them cry for their mothers – it's a small price to pay to rid the world of scum like him.'

We fell silent and she began to look slightly anxious. 'What's up?' I asked.

'He's on the run and this is the place he'll come to. He'll realize the game is up, so he's got nothing to lose.'

'Are you going to ring the local police?'

She shook her head. 'No, they'll come here mob-handed and someone will warn him off.'

'So, what do we do?'

'The only thing we can do. Wait for him.'

Twenty-Seven

We sat half concealed behind a curtain, staring out on to heavy rain for two hours waiting for him.

Now that I knew Helen's true mission she wanted to talk. Far from being a professional photographer, she was a mere amateur. It had provided the ideal cover for her activities. After she'd left school she'd gone to university to read criminology.

'Why keep it a secret?' I asked.

'It wasn't exactly a secret but I'd only kept in touch with Gill from school and I knew if I told her I wanted to join the police graduate entry scheme she'd take the piss because she always thought I was a bit on the wimpy side. Plus, if I failed, I didn't want her to know. Once I'd got my degree I was fast-tracked and now I'm an inspector but I plan to make superintendent.'

I was impressed. Helen had always been very feminine but she obviously had real guts and determination. And she could lie as well as any psychopath.

'All that and you're married too?'

'Yes.'

'Do you want to talk about it?'

'Not really. It's hard. We don't see much of each other and we're nearly always in some sort of danger.'

'At least it's not boring.'

'Sometimes boring would be heaven. This isn't the sort of job anyone can do for long. In fact I've been told to take a year off undercover work and I may not be allowed to be connected with paedophile crimes again.'

'Why's that?'

'After a long time you get hardened to it. It's blatant and in your face and your initial repulsion turns more towards acceptance. You find you begin to sympathize with the perpetrators...' She broke off. 'Don't get me wrong, Warrinder isn't sexually interested in children. He's into money and power – that's what turns him on. The really scary thing is that he seems so normal. He's been kind and gentle towards me. He's treated me like a princess. He's played with my mind.'

I guessed at this point in her assignment she was beginning to get screwed up. It's one thing to live with a cruel, unfeeling monster and know exactly how he'll react to circumstances, quite another to live with a dual personality, knowing that the dark side is there just below the surface.

It was about two thirty when we heard the

rumble of a lorry. I peeped out to see a brewery lorry, on the back of which were a few wooden barrels and several smaller metal barrels. The driver stopped and sat in his cab smoking a cigarette. Helen was on her feet.

'Hold on,' I said. 'He might be waiting for Warrinder. Let's get up to the attic. He might come in to check on you – if he comes alone we might be able to overpower him.'

'It might just be a delivery,' she said.

'No,' I said, pulling her towards the door. 'I think that Alison is in one of those barrels. And they want to remove the evidence.'

Helen clapped a hand over her mouth. 'But there couldn't be anything in the barrels – there was brandy in one and sherry in the other.'

'There's a trick involved somewhere,' I said, trying to sound convincing. 'I'm sure she's in one of the barrels.'

From the attic we could just about see the lorry but we couldn't see the driver. We'd been watching for a few minutes when a car drew up and out stepped Warrinder and Trenchard. They began talking to the driver, still in his cab. We couldn't handle three men – it was ridiculous. 'Let's call the police,' I said.

Helen shook her head. 'By the time they get here they'll be gone. He can't be allowed to escape this time.'

295

'Well, we can't just stay here and watch them go.'

'I don't intend to. Warrinder wanted me dead, so maybe my cover is already blown. He'll come looking to make sure I'm still locked in here and to finish me off if I'm not already dead.'

'I still think we should call the local police.'

'Yeah. OK,' she said reluctantly.

I'd just started rooting in my shoulder bag for my mobile phone when we heard footsteps. 'Too bloody late,' I muttered. Helen signalled for me to stand behind the door. I looked in vain for a weapon. What was I supposed to do – trip him up? Helen got on the floor and lay on her side looking towards the door. 'When he's inside,' she whispered, 'take the key from the outside and lock us all in.'

The footsteps became louder and it sounded as if there was only one of them. I began to tremble. Warrinder was young, fit and strong. Helen may have been a policewoman but she was slight and if it came to a fight I imagined she'd be fast and nimble but no great shakes at fending off a sharp left hook. As for me, I'd rather try to talk my way out. I could be brave as long as I didn't even try to think about the consequences. Once I thought blood and loosened teeth, my insides turned to jelly.

The key turned in the lock. As he slowly

opened the door, I could see him in the space between the door and the frame. He stared at Helen lying on the floor and then half turned as if satisfied. It could have only been seconds but it seemed longer, because he changed his mind, turned and put one foot into the room. I sharply slammed the door in his face. He staggered backwards and then righted himself and charged into the room like an enraged bull. I was backing away terrified when a punch caught me in the jaw. I was aware of falling and then Helen's voice saying, 'Hands up you bastard.' The world was spinning but I saw the gun in her hand. He kicked the gun away and the shot reverberated round the room, loud as a cannon. It landed near me and I made a grab for it but he too lunged for it at the same time. Helen had dived on to his back and was yanking back his head by the hair. But he had the gun and it was aimed at me. He was momentarily distracted by the sound of the lorry's engine starting up. I kicked him between the legs. Helen was still hanging on to him like a monkey and now had an arm around his neck. It made no difference. He shot me.

A red-hot poker entered my left arm and stayed there. I don't know if I screamed but things became very black as I fell to the floor. I was vaguely aware of the sound of footsteps, scuffling and shouting, but the only thing that seemed real was the searing pain in my arm.

Helen's face came into view as she bent down to tell me the ambulance was on its way, and when I next squinted around I was alone and blood was steadily trickling down to my fingertips. I heard another two shots being fired. How long I was left alone I don't know, but I knew I was both frightened and outraged. I held up my left arm with my right to lessen the blood flow and managed to get to my feet. It was slow progress but I managed to get down the stairs. I was aware I was leaving a trail of blood but I didn't care. For all I knew, he'd shot Helen too.

Outside, I was staggering around when the ambulance and the police arrived. I slumped to the ground and saw a pool of blood gathering around me. Just before an oxygen mask was placed over my nose and mouth, I looked into the blue eyes of a uniformed PC. He supported my shoulders as the paramedics struggled to find a vein to put up an intravenous infusion. 'I'm Mark,' he said. 'Don't go to sleep. You're going to be just fine.' I tried to focus on his face. When I did finally get him into focus, I saw that apart from largish ears he was very attractive and I reasoned that if I could still work that out I wasn't quite at death's door. I clung on to his hand and begged him not to leave me.

So he stayed with me in the ambulance

and during my time in the A&E department. He was still there whilst I was having my third unit of blood. By then I knew his life story and that he was free and single. I'd been given an injection for the pain and the euphoria was such that I even saw being shot through a rosy glow. It wasn't so bad. My silver lining was the lovely Mark sitting beside me, holding my hand and hanging on to my every word.

I remembered little about the operation on my arm but, when I came round from the anaesthetic, Mark was still there and I wondered why. I began to feel anxious. Where was Helen? Had they caught Warrinder? 'Are you here to protect me?' I slurred at Mark.

'It's my day off. I've chosen to spend it looking after you.'

'Thanks a million,' I said as I drifted back to a warm and cosy sleep.

Helen visited me the next day and I was well enough to ask questions. Warrinder had escaped ... in a way. He'd run towards the beach pursued by Helen and Robert Roberts, who'd been in the area – 'snooping', Helen called it. But he hadn't taken the path to the beach, he'd taken the cliff-top path and just kept on running.

'I feel cheated,' said Helen. 'He's dead but in a way that doesn't help. He should have stood trial.'

She looked pale and upset. 'You need a

good long holiday,' I said.

'I'm taking one. I'm resigning from the force. I want my marriage to work and I don't think it will if I have to associate with any more low life. Nigel didn't think he'd play the jealous husband but knowing I slept with Warrinder has affected him. It's affected us both.'

'You're worn out. Take a holiday together, somewhere exotic. You may feel differently when you get back.'

'I don't think so. There is something else ... have you been interviewed by the police yet?'

'Today sometime, so Mark told me.'

'That gun wasn't legal,' she murmured. 'Nigel insisted I had one. If SO5 finds out I'll be dismissed.'

'I only saw Warrinder with a gun and that's what I'll say.'

'Thanks, Kate. I'd rather resign than get the push.'

'What about Jamie?' I asked.

'Jamie and Trenchard have sung like canaries. They were the chief henchmen. And Trenchard himself is a paedophile. I hope he rots in prison.'

'And the barrels?'

'You were right, Kate. It was horrific – Alison had been chopped in half, wrapped in formaldehyde-soaked sheets then encased in strong plastic. Warrinder needed help, of course – he paid a vast sum to a local cooper.

He'd rigged up a foil bag, just like the ones in wine boxes, so that, when the tap was opened, out came the sherry and the brandy. Of course, no one carried on until the bag was empty.'

'Was she killed in the cellar?' I asked.

'I'm not sure. Cause of death seems to be strangulation. The three of them, Warrinder, the estate agent from hell and the cooper, sawed her in half and then stuffed her body into the barrels. They cleaned up the cellar floor – leaving just the one clue – the contact lens. I think Fran found it or maybe she'd already found the other one in another room, and she either confronted him or decided she couldn't carry on living, knowing that her husband and the father of her children was a monster.'

I was beginning to feel tired now, and my arm throbbed, but I still wanted to talk and, even though the ward manager passed by my bed showing me five fingers, I didn't want to be hurried. 'I suppose the only consolation,' I said, waving cheerfully at the ward manager, 'is that a major paedophile ring has been broken and that's down to you, Helen. You risked your life, because if he'd found out you were working undercover you'd be dead.'

She shrugged. 'That's the nature of the job. Anyway, you've had your share of altercations.'

'How do you know that?'

'I didn't meet you by accident. It was a set-up. Gill didn't know what was going on but the cheque she gave you wasn't her money. SO5 paid indirectly. I told her I wanted you to investigate the so-called "ghosts" but it was to be a secret between Gill and me that I paid.'

'Why Gill and me?'

'We checked out a few school friends. Gill was an obvious choice, because we'd stayed in touch. Paul would have been suspicious if I didn't invite a few friends. Gill just got too involved and I had to try to put her off, hence the row, but she was dogged and she died because she couldn't let go.' She managed a half smile and patted my hand. 'And you, because you knew nothing about me and in a crisis you could have proved useful. You should be flattered. The police thought your investigation clear-up rates were pretty good.'

I didn't know what to say to that. But one other thing did trouble me. 'Tell me your secret,' I said. 'How did you get Warrinder not only to trust you but to fall in love with you and want to marry you?'

She was about to reveal all when Mark walked in. 'I'll tell you another time,' she said. 'And thanks for taking the bullet for me.'

I was disappointed all round. Warrinder

had avoided a trial and prison and I'd been denied her feminine secrets.

'Hey, come on, cheer up,' said Mark as he kissed my hand. 'I'm taking some annual leave so that I can drive you back to Longborough.'

My disappointment left me as abruptly as a rainbow fades. Whatever 'secrets' Helen had, I wasn't doing so badly.

It was that night, listening on the hospital headphones to the news, that I heard the antidepressant drug 'Tourine' had been taken off the market. People already taking it were advised to see their GPs. One of the side effects, it seemed, was to increase depression in some people. Six people had committed suicide whilst on the drug.

The death of Fran and her children would always remain a mystery now, for the one man who was most likely to know the cause had taken the easy way out. My consolation was to also hear on the news that a major paedophile ring had been broken and that several young Argentinian children had been rescued from a semi-derelict house in South London.

Two days later I was back in Longborough. I hadn't told Hubert I'd been shot. He'd have come dashing down to Cornwall and he couldn't afford the time or the worry. He saw me from his office, being helped out of a car, and came out to meet me.

'What have you done?' he said, seeing my arm in a sling.

'I've only been shot,' I said. 'It's not major.'

'Well, I call it major. Another cock-up, was it?'

'No! We got a result.'

'That makes a change. Welcome home.' He looked questioningly at Mark. I made the introductions and we went upstairs to Hubert's kitchen, where he began busily making us a meal. Jasper was delirious with excitement, although most of it was reserved for Mark.

Mark had gone to the bathroom when Hubert put an arm around me and said, 'You do realize he is a toy boy. He's years younger than you are.'

'Yes, I know. I'm in the first throes of love. Great, isn't it?'

'I'm going to lose you one of these days,' he said sadly.

'We'll see,' I said, giving him a peck on the cheek. 'I'm on a roll at the moment though, Hubert. Men seem to be clamouring for me.'

'It won't last.'

I didn't let his pessimism affect me. Instead I felt a real surge of optimism. I'd stopped a bullet, found an attractive man or two, and once my arm was better there would be no stopping me, in life or in the bedroom.